The Patsy

A Comedy in Three Acts

by Barry Conners

A SAMUEL FRENCH ACTING EDITION

SAMUEL FRENCH

FOUNDED 1830

New York Hollywood London Toronto

SAMUELFRENCH.COM

ISBN   978-0-573-61376-0   Printed   in   U.S.A.   #18037

THE PATSY

Produced at the Apollo Theatre, Shaftesbury Avenue, London, December 19th, 1928, with the following cast of characters :—

(In the order of their appearance.)

MRS. WILLIAM HARRINGTON .	.	.	.	.	.	*Lucia Moore.*
BILL HARRINGTON	.	.	.	.	.	. *Frank Shannon.*
GRACE HARRINGTON	.	.	.	.	.	. *Leonore Sorsby.*
PATRICIA HARRINGTON .	.	.	.	.	.	. *Helen Ford.*
BILLY CALDWELL .	.	.	.	.	.	. *Kenneth Loane.*
TONY ANDERSON .	.	.	.	.	.	. *Alexander Clark.*

SADIE BUCHANAN.

FRANCIS PATRICK O'FLAHERTY.

"TRIP" BUSTY.

SYNOPSIS OF SCENES

ACT   I.—Living-room of the HARRINGTON home. Evening.

ACT II.—Same. Next Monday evening.

ACT III.—Same. The Friday night following.

The Play produced by GEORGE D. PARKER.

NOTE

The Characters of

SADIE BUCHANAN

FRANCIS PATRICK O'FLAHERTY

and

" TRIP " BUSTY

can be omitted without interfering with the plot of the play.
Folios 47–48, 49–50, 67–68.

THE PATSY

ACT I

SCENE.—*The Living-room of the* HARRINGTONS', *in a medium-sized town. Evening—after dinner.*

Up stage C. *is a broad staircase leading off* R. *to the upper story. Down stage* L. *from this is a door leading to the dining-room and the rear of the house. Large windows* L. *looking out upon a yard where trees screen the light of a distant street lamp. Down* R. *is the large front door with glass panels on either side.*

The room is painted a light cream colour with trimmings to match in the modern style. The house is new—or, at least, newly decorated. The furniture and furnishings denote a middle-class family in well-to-do circumstances.

Down R. *of* C. *is a large couch, overstuffed and attractive. There is a table behind it. The telephone is on the* R. *of this table. There is a lamp on the baby-grand piano* L. *An upholstered arm-chair up* L.C. *Arm-chair down* L.C. *Other chairs are about the room.*

Books, etc., about stage. Standard lamp up R. *Cupboard covered by chintz is in flat* L. *of stairs for hats, etc. Baby-grand piano or small table between window and door* L. *Large window* R. *above front door with seat inset. Vases of flowers about stage.*

The whole effect should be attractive and comfortable, but not luxurious.

(See Photograph of Scene.)

AT RISE : *The stage is unoccupied.*

After a moment, the door-bell rings. There is no immediate response. Bell rings again. MRS. HARRINGTON *enters and comes downstairs.*

MRS. HARRINGTON *is a woman of about 48 or 49. She is tall, plump, very good-looking, and with an air and manner of some surface culture. She is dressed in evening clothes, but without the outdoor wraps.*

MRS. HARRINGTON *is of the peevish, overbearing type. She considers herself a martyr and is apparently unaware that her unreasonable and petulant behaviour is responsible for most of her troubles.*

She comes down the stairs angrily—arranging her hair as though having been interrupted in the act of dressing. She runs to small mirror up R. *and looks at herself, patting and smoothing her hair before answering door-bell. She moves round in front of settee and opens the street door down* R.

Mr. BILL HARRINGTON *is discovered.*

HARRINGTON (POP) *is a tall, stout, round-faced, ruddy man with a somewhat sporty get-up in clothes. He is the hail-fellow-well-met type—has a hearty laugh and is usually in high spirits—but can talk back with force and directness when annoyed. He carries a brand-new alligator-hide bag, large and expensive looking, and a brief-case. He carries also, on his arm, a light raincoat and an umbrella.*

POP (*stands in the door a moment with a wide smile and bright*). Here's mamma's baby boy !

MRS. HARRINGTON (*turning away to* R.C., *very annoyed*). Well, for Heaven's sake ! Did you make me come all the way down here just to open the door for you ? Haven't you got your latchkey ?

POP (*entering and taking her in his arms*). I wanted to surprise you. How's my best girl ? (*He hugs her to him and kisses her.*)

MRS. HARRINGTON. Bill ! Don't muss my hair, will you ? I just got through fixing it. (*She is peeved.*)

POP. What do I care about your old hair ? How's my sweet mamma ? All fixed up pretty ? Going some place ?

MRS. HARRINGTON (*snaps*). You know very well this is my Bridge Club night. What happened ? How'd you get home so soon ? You haven't lost your job, have you ?

POP. Lost my job ! What are you talking about ? No ! (*Throwing his raincoat over her arm and handing umbrella, she takes up to cupboard* L.C., *then taking things out of the new bag which he has placed on settee.*) I worked eighteen hours yesterday and made four towns and sixteen the day before and made three. Saved the firm two days' expenses. (*Handing box of candy to her.*)

MRS. HARRINGTON. You worked all that time in two days ? I wouldn't think of such a thing !

POP. Neither would I. The boss thought of it.

MRS. HARRINGTON (*seeing his new bag*). When did you get that bag ?

POP (*holding up bag*). Got it yesterday. Real alligator skin. Ain't it a beauty ?

MRS. HARRINGTON. Your old one was good enough, wasn't it ?

POP. Aw, listen, May—I had a little luck. If my constituents eat all the groceries I sold the last three weeks the weight reducers are going to be living on the fat of the land.

MRS. HARRINGTON (*setting her lips primly*). Did you have supper ?

POP (*shutting and putting bag on chair up* R.). Yeah—don't worry —I had dinner on the diner.

MRS. HARRINGTON (*crosses to suitcase*). Yes, and I suppose it cost you four or five dollars, too.

Pop. No, it didn't cost four or five dollars. (*At clothes cupboard up* L.C.) And what if it did ? The firm's paying for it, ain't they ?

Mrs. Harrington. Well, I'm glad you had a lucky trip—it happened just in time. (*Miserably, sitting on settee.*)

Pop. What do you mean—just in time ? That sounds like bad news. (*Crosses to table* R.C., *behind settee.*)

Mrs. Harrington (*firmly.* Pop *lights cigar*). Now that Grace is engaged to Billy Caldwell you've got to get another car.

Pop (*getting angry and coming down* C.). Now don't start that ! I got rid of my car and I'm going to stay that way.

Mrs. Harrington. Oh, no, you're not !

Pop. Oh, yes, I am. I ain't going to try to support a family and an automobile and the Government all on one income. We're not going to get another car.

Mrs. Harrington (*with great sarcasm*). So ! You're going to be idiotic again, are you ?

Pop. That's right ! Go ahead and insult me—(*moving away to* L. *and back again to* C.)—so that I'll feel at home !

Mrs. Harrington. We've got to have a car. (*Rising.*) Grace is making a brilliant marriage and you're not going to ruin it by making us all look like a lot of paupers.

Pop. Brilliant marriage, eh ? Listen, May—the only brilliant marriage that ever happened in this family was when you married me. (*Crossing away to* L. *and turning.*)

Mrs. Harrington (*witheringly*). You're more idiotic than you ever were.

Pop. Maybe I am. What does that prove ?

Mrs. Harrington. It proves that nothing is impossible. Why don't you pick up your things ? (*Picks up dressing-gown which* Pop *has taken out of bag and placed on settee.*)

Pop. All right. I'm telling you that the only way for a poor man to get on his feet is to get rid of his car. I've been down and out for the last time. (*Moving up* C. *to staircase.*)

Mrs. Harrington (*sitting again on settee*). If you were any kind of a father you'd be glad to be down and out if your daughter could marry somebody like Billy Caldwell. You can go out and spend money on yourself——

Pop (*up* C.). No, I ain't been spending any money on myself. But listen, May—I'm getting old. I can't sell groceries all my life. I've got to save something and invest it.

Mrs. Harrington (*sarcastically, sitting back on settee*). Yes—so you can buy some more lots in Florida, I suppose.

Pop (*furiously, at the top of his voice, moving down* C.). Good Lord ! Ain't you never going to forget them damned lots in Florida ?

Mrs. Harrington (*taking out her handkerchief and crying*). What are the Caldwells going to think of us ? Here I am going to the bridge club—and instead of having a car like everybody else I've got to ride in the street-car like a common washerwoman. (*Facing away to* R.)

POP. There's just as good people as you are riding in street-cars.

MRS. HARRINGTON (*rising*). You just seem possessed to do everything you can to make people think we're a lot of paupers with the wolf at the door.

POP (*hurt*). If any wolf comes to the door while you're here he'd better look out or he'll be a brand-new fur rug.

MRS. HARRINGTON (*crossing and sitting on arm-chair* L.C.). Every time we try to amount to something or be somebody——

POP (*interrupting*). You know what's the matter with you, don't you? You're going crazy on the subject of society. If you had your way you'd be taking your meals at the First National Bank and getting your washing done at the post-office. (*Sitting on settee.*)

MRS. HARRINGTON (*crying softly and facing away to* L.). Everybody we know has got a car——

POP (*rising—angrily*). Wait a minute! I've been away three weeks! I walk into the house and you start the same old stuff. You're getting me so I hate to come home, May.

MRS. HARRINGTON (*crying a little louder*). Even our washerwoman's husband has a car!

POP (*glares at her*). Listen, May, for twenty-five years you've been weeping! Every time you want to win an argument you burst into spring weather! But from now on I'm going to be a hard-boiled Humpty-Dumpty. (*Crossing down* R. *and turning.*) Go ahead and cry! See if you can win this battle. (*Walks up and down.*)

MRS. HARRINGTON. You don't care what people think of us—you never did. (*Weeps copiously, a little louder.*)

POP. Go ahead—put on the old record and start the phonograph!

MRS. HARRINGTON (*weeps furiously*). Oh! Oh!

POP (*at the top of his voice as he crosses up* C.). Go on—bawl your head off. I'm used to it. (*Quite quietly as he turns back.*) But listen to me, May. When I'm dying my last words are going to be as follows: You got just as much chance of me buying another automobile as you have of seeing a Swiss battleship sinking in the Sahara desert.

GRACE (*upstairs, calling from off stage*). Who's that, Mother?

POP (*change comes over him—he turns, smiling and leaning on the newel of the stairs*). It's me.

GRACE (*upstairs*). Is that you, Billy?

POP (*smiling*). Not the Billy you mean. Come on down, Beautiful.

GRACE (*upstairs*). Is that you, Father?

POP. Yeah. Come on down here. (*Moving away to* L.)

(Enter GRACE, downstairs. GRACE is a tall, very beautiful girl of about 24, dressed in evening clothes—also without street wrap. She is selfish, cold, and petulant, excepting when she has a purpose in being pleasant.)

GRACE (C.). Hello, Father. How'd you get home so soon?

POP. Oh, just a little luck making connections. *(He moves up to C. and holds her off with both hands and smiles at her. Looks at her ring.)* Well, Grace, it's a beauty. How does it seem to be engaged?

GRACE. You got my letter then?

POP. Sure.

GRACE. Were you very surprised?

POP. Well, I've got to admit I was—a little. It all happened kind of sudden, didn't it?

GRACE. I don't know that it did. *(Coming down stage a little.)*

(POP is now between the two.)

What's the matter? Don't you like Billy Caldwell?

POP *(slightly above them)*. Why—sure—as much as I've seen of him. I don't know him—only to say hello to him.

MRS. HARRINGTON *(amazed)*. Great heavens! Are you objecting to him?

POP. No. Only I always kind of thought you and Tony Anderson might get married.

GRACE *(with a despairing look at her mother)*. Tony Anderson! *(Crossing down and sitting L. of settee R.C.)*

MRS. HARRINGTON. You're not comparing Tony Anderson with Billy Caldwell, are you?

POP *(looks at them both, surprised)*. Tony Anderson was good enough to spend his money on her for four years. What's the matter with him?

GRACE *(snappishly)*. I don't love him. That's what's the matter with him.

POP. Well, that's what I mean. You changed your mind kinda sudden, didn't you?

MRS. HARRINGTON *(moving closer to GRACE on sofa)*. She had a right to change her mind, hadn't she?

POP. Sure she had. But do you think Billy Caldwell will make her as good a husband as Tony? That's the question.

GRACE. I think that's something for me to decide, isn't it? Tony Anderson hasn't got any more money than Billy Caldwell has.

POP. Listen! I ain't putting up any arguments. You're going to marry Caldwell—and it's O.K. with me. Only I can't help feeling a little bit sorry for Tony—that's all. You might not love him—but he certainly is in love with you.

GRACE *(coldly and finally)*. Well, I'm going to marry Billy Caldwell.

Mrs. Harrington (*rising and crossing up* L.). Don't drop those ashes on the floor.

(Pop *up* c. *rubs foot on floor.*)

Pop. Well, listen, Grace—whoever you marry, I hope you're going to be very happy. (*Turning away.*) Only what was the matter with Tony ?

Mrs. Harrington. He doesn't dance—he doesn't play bridge

———

Grace. All he can do is sit around like a bump on a log and talk psychology. And besides, I despise a man who thinks he understands women.

Pop (*knocking cigar ash on tray, table* R.C.). Huh ! You ought to feel sorry for him.

Grace. Listen, Father, Billy Caldwell is calling for me to-night —and I wish you'd—you'd——

Pop (*looking at her keenly*). Wish I'd what ?

Grace (*hesitating*). Well—don't tell him any travelling salesman stories—and watch your language when he's here. Don't say " I ain't " and " seen and done it " and things like that—he wouldn't understand.

Pop (*stiffening and looking at her narrowly*). Oh ! (*Pause.*) Yeah ! I got you. (*Turning away.*)

Grace (*rising*). Oh, now I suppose you're going to misunderstand !

Pop (*turning back again*). No, I ain't going to misunderstand at all ! You're going to marry one of the Caldwells so you're just a little bit ashamed of your old man, because he has to go out and peddle groceries. I got you.

Grace (*rising*). Nothing of the sort ! (*Moving up* R. *behind table.*)

Pop. Well, listen, Grace, if it wasn't for them groceries I'm peddling you wouldn't have nothing to eat on the table.

Mrs. Harrington. Them groceries. (*With a sneer as she crosses to settee and sits.*) That's the sort of language she's talking about. She's just trying to make a decent impression, that's all.

Grace (*angrily*). Oh, what's the use of talking, Mother ? If he insists on misinterpreting my meaning——

Pop. Well, this is a hot one. What a wonderful home-coming this turned out to be ! (*Sits on chair* L.C.)

Grace (*glares at him*). I'll be glad when I'm out of this house ! (*She wheels and starts for stairs.*)

Pop. I could make a snappy answer to that one, too.

Grace (*turning at the stairs and facing him*). Well, go ahead and make it.

Mrs. Harrington (*rising, loudly to* Pop). Uh uh uh—you've said enough !

Pop (*glaring at* Grace). Yes, maybe I have.

(Mrs. Harrington *sits again on settee.*)

Grace (*with a nasty smile. On stairs*). Ah, Mother, has he heard about Patricia ?

Pop (*suddenly very interested*). What about Patricia ? Where is she ?

Grace (*to her mother*). Well, you'd better tell him. (*Sneeringly to her father.*) It makes a lot of difference when it's something about Patricia, doesn't it ?

Pop (*glaring at her*). That's a pretty tough one to take from you, Grace. I've treated you pretty well the last twenty-four years.

(Grace *is about to speak.*)

Mrs. Harrington (*rising. To Grace*). Uh, uh, uh. You've had enough to say, too. You shut your mouth and go upstairs.

(*Exit* Grace *upstairs.* Pop *stares after her angrily up the stairs a moment and then looks at* Mrs. Harrington, *and slowly comes down to her.*)

Pop (*moving down to L. of settee*). Listen, May—what's all the use of fighting like this ? It's getting worse all the time. Let's cut it out—what do you say, old girl ? We've been through too many tough times together. We don't hate each other. What do you say ? (*His tone and manner are kindness itself.*)

Mrs. Harrington (*rising and crossing to L.C. Haughtily*). Well, who started it ?

Pop (*instantly loud and furious*). I suppose I did ?

Mrs. Harrington. Well, who did ?

Pop. Never mind who started it. You make me tired.—What did Grace mean about Pat ? What's the matter ? Where is she ?

Mrs. Harrington (*worried, sitting on chair L.C.*). Bill, I don't know whether she's in some terrible trouble—or whether she's losing her mind !

Pop (*sitting on R. of the settee. Genuinely worried*). Losing her mind ! Why ? What's happened ?

Mrs. Harrington. A lot of queer things.

Pop. What do you mean ?

Mrs. Harrington. Well, to begin with—she's having dinner to-night with that big fat Mr. O'Flaherty.

Pop. What O'Flaherty ?

Mrs. Harrington. That lawyer.

Pop. Oh, you mean O'Flaherty of Rosenbloom and O'Flaherty ?

Mrs. Harrington. Yes. He's old enough to be her father— she's had dinner with him twice before this week. She told us she was going to Aunt Margaret's.

Pop. Where did she dine with him ?

Mrs. Harrington. At the Garfield Hotel.

Pop. How do you know ?

MRS. HARRINGTON. Grace found out. She knows the head waiter there.

POP. Did you say anything to her?

MRS. HARRINGTON. She doesn't know we know it.

POP. Is that why you think she's in trouble—or is that why you think she's losing her mind?

MRS. HARRINGTON. I think she's in trouble because every time the door-bell rings she dashes upstairs and hides. I think she's done something and she's afraid someone is coming here to tell on her.

POP. That does sound like she was in trouble. Maybe that's why she's seeing the lawyer. But what makes you think she is losing her mind?

MRS. HARRINGTON. Well, when she gets home I want you to listen to the way she talks. I hate to say it, Bill—but I'm afraid something has happened to her mind. (*Touching her forehead.*)

POP. What does she say?

MRS. HARRINGTON. For the last two weeks she's been going around saying not to cry in the milk because there's tears in it.

POP (*dumbfounded*). Not to cry in the milk because there's tears in it? Who does she say it to, the milkman?

MRS. HARRINGTON. No, she says it to everybody. And when she gets tired saying that she goes around saying that everybody is a stage-hand.

POP (*flabbergasted*). Everybody is a stage-hand! (*Shaking his head as if he did not believe it.*)

MRS. HARRINGTON. Well, you wait till you hear her. Every time Grace or I open our mouths she says something that isn't connected with the conversation at all—something perfectly idiotic.

POP (*worried*). Oh, yeh!

MRS. HARRINGTON. Four times in the last two weeks I've caught her with her door locked at five o'clock in the morning walking around her room talking to herself and laughing.

POP (*astonished*). Laughing?

MRS. HARRINGTON. Yes. She walks around the room talking to herself and then she laughs.

POP. Maybe something's tickling her.

MRS. HARRINGTON (*rising and moving down and sitting on other end of sofa*). Well, there's always been some worry about her since the day she was born—now I suppose we're going to have this!

POP (*pause*). You know, somehow, I've never worried about Pat.

MRS. HARRINGTON. Well, I have.

POP. Oh, she gets into a lot of trouble. But I've always taught her to do the sportsmanlike thing and you have got to admit she always tries to do it.

MRS. HARRINGTON. H'm! You can call it that if you want to—but it's just been a mystery to me. (*Rising. Crosses behind table by L. of the settee.*)

Pop (*follows her by the* ʀ. *end of settee—they meet at* ᴏ. *of table above settee*). Well, you don't understand her, May. You never did understand her. Besides you can't blame her for not coming to you—because every time there's any trouble between her and Grace you always stick up for Grace.

Mʀs. Hᴀʀʀɪɴɢᴛᴏɴ. That isn't so !

Pop (*firmly, moving down* ʀ. *below sofa*). Yes, it is, and you know it. You've got her so she's just like a stranger in the house—and it's your fault.

Mʀs. Hᴀʀʀɪɴɢᴛᴏɴ. If there's anything wrong with her it's the way you brought her up. (*Crossing to* ᴏ.)

Pop. Is that so ? (*Moving to front of settee*.) Well, I'm not going to let you get away with that ! Every time somebody says something nice about the girls you raised them. And every time there's any trouble I raised them. (*Sitting on settee again.*)

Mʀs. Hᴀʀʀɪɴɢᴛᴏɴ (*after* Pop *sits*). Yes ! Whose fault was it she joined the Country Club where there's drinking and everything else going on ?

Pop. Why shouldn't she join the Country Club ? She's nineteen years old and it's time she got out and met some young people her own age.

Mʀs. Hᴀʀʀɪɴɢᴛᴏɴ. She could meet them right here if she wanted to—but she won't. Boys invite her to places and she won't go with them. And they ask her if they can call and she won't let them. She's always been that way, and you know it. (*Sitting on chair* ʟ.ᴄ.)

Pop (*rising and moving up to stairs, then coming down to* ᴏ. *to* ʟ.). Oh, Lord ! Every time I come home there's some new trouble worse than the last one. You don't really think there's anything really wrong with her head, do you ?

Mʀs. Hᴀʀʀɪɴɢᴛᴏɴ. Well, it wouldn't be any great surprise to me. You know your cousin Egbert wasn't any too sensible.

Pop. My cousin Egbert, huh ? Well, how about your Uncle Johnnie on your father's side ? If there's any insanity in the family it didn't come from my side.

Mʀs. Hᴀʀʀɪɴɢᴛᴏɴ. My Uncle Johnnie got kicked by a horse—in the head—that's the reason he was—odd.

Pop. Just the same, when he was forty-nine years old he invented the idea of taking a bath—and he thought it was something new. (*Turns up* ᴏ.)

(Mʀs. Hᴀʀʀɪɴɢᴛᴏɴ *turns and glares at him, speechless.*)

Mʀs. Hᴀʀʀɪɴɢᴛᴏɴ. Oh, hush !

(*Enter* Pᴀᴛʀɪᴄɪᴀ *from the front door* ʀ. Pᴀᴛʀɪᴄɪᴀ *is a girl smaller than* Gʀᴀᴄᴇ, *with a bright, pretty face, a vivacious style, and a likeable and spirited personality. She is dressed in snappy street costume. She stops short suddenly on seeing her father, leaning back against the door, and a wide delighted smile spreads over her face.*)

PATRICIA. Well, if it isn't that old sweetheart of mine. (*She goes to him with outstretched arms.*) Hello, Pops! (*Jumping into his arms,* POP *holding her in the air at arm's length and kissing her.*) Gee! I'm glad you're home. I've just missed you something terrible! (*She kisses him again.*)

POP (*hugs her to him with unusual tenderness*). How are you, Baby? (*He pats her a little—then he holds her off and looks at her with a sort of worried curiosity.*) How are you feeling?

PATRICIA (*notices his worried look*). Fine! What's the matter, Pop? (*She turns, peeping round her father and taking a nervous look at her mother.*)

POP. Have you been a good girl while I was gone?

PATRICIA (*senses she has been talked about and gives her mother another swift glance. She then breaks into a wide smile*). What are you trying to do, Pop? Make a liar out of me?

POP. What you been doing?

PATRICIA (*hesitates and then shakes her head*). Nope, I'd better not tell. Open confession is good for the soul—but it's dog-goned hard on the reputation.

POP (*looks at her, worried, and then glances at* MRS. HARRINGTON, *who gives him a look and turns away*). Huh?

PATRICIA (*eagerly—to change the subject. Crossing up* L. *to cupboard and hanging up her hat, then moving down* C.). Oh, Pop! I've been so busy, I'm all out of breath. You know that Mr. Eisenwein, who owns the department store?

POP. Yes?

PATRICIA. Well, he has offered a silver cup to any lady of the Country Club who can correctly name the three Americans who have done the most for this country musically, politically, and financially. And I think I'm going to win it.

MRS. HARRINGTON (*rising*). Why don't you stay out of that contest? You know Grace is trying to win that cup.

PATRICIA (*turning to her mother*). Grace hasn't a chance to win that cup.

MRS. HARRINGTON (*peevishly*). Well, never mind Mr. Eisenwein and his cup. Where have you been? (*Crossing over to* R. *of sofa.*)

PATRICIA (*turns as if to speak and suddenly shuts her mouth*). What's that?

MRS. HARRINGTON. I want to know where you were until this hour?

PATRICIA (*sitting on sofa next to* MRS. HARRINGTON). Well—(*hesitating*)—what would you say if I told you I was at Aunt Margaret's?

MRS. HARRINGTON. I'd say it was an untruth—I know better.

PATRICIA. Then that's exactly what I'm not going to tell you. (*Smiling broadly at* POP, *who is on her* L.)

MRS. HARRINGTON. Where were you?

PATRICIA. Well—— (*Hesitating—then has a sudden thought.*) Do you know where I was?

Mrs. Harrington. You answer me ! I want to know where you were.

Patricia. Well, now, wait a minute. (*Smiling.*) If you're going to be very particular about this you've got to give me time to think of a good one.

Mrs. Harrington. What ?

Patricia. You want me to tell you something you can believe, don't you ?

Mrs. Harrington. Yes—and you're going to tell me—or as big as you are I'll take a slipper to you !

(Patricia *turns and grins widely at* Pop.)

Pop (*crossing to sofa and sitting on her* L.). Now look here, Pat, you've been away from home for dinner three times this last week——

(*All three are seated on sofa.*)

Patricia (*shocked—to* Mrs. Harrington). Aw, Ma, did you tell Pop that ?

Mrs. Harrington. I certainly did !

Patricia (*with a gesture of resignation*). Well, I'm sorry you did —but there's no use crying over spilt milk because there's enough water in it already. (*Leaning back.*)

Pop (*exchanges worried look across* Patricia *with* Mrs. Harrington). Huh ! What do you mean by that ?

Patricia. Pops, I didn't know you and Ma were going to be worried about it. It isn't fair to make you worry. So I suppose the sportsmanlike thing to do is to tell you where I was.

Mrs. Harrington. Where ?

Patricia. I had dinner three nights this week at the Garfield Hotel with Francis Patrick O'Flaherty, of Rosenbloom and O'Flaherty.

Pop. How'd you get acquainted with him ?

Patricia. Ladies' Night at the Elks Club.

Mrs. Harrington (*angrily*). What business have you going to dinner with him ?

Patricia (*appealingly to* Pop). It's going to be a surprise— please don't make me tell, Pop.

Pop. You're not in any trouble, are you ?

Patricia (*starts and looks worried*). Trouble—no ! Uh-huh. I— I just want to surprise you. In fact, if it turns out right you will probably be startled—same as if your grandpa went to kiss you and bit your ear. (*Sitting back and laughing.*)

(Pop *and* Mrs. Harrington *exchange another worried look.* Mrs. Harrington *rises and crosses by* R., *behind table.*)

Pop. Huh ?

Patricia. You'd be surprised to see my name in all the papers, wouldn't you ?

MRS. HARRINGTON (*with great meaning, up almost* C.). Well—I wouldn't!

PATRICIA (*hurt, winces a little and looks at her mother rather wistfully*). Oh, Ma, I'm just trying to do something so you'll be proud of me.

MRS. HARRINGTON (*cuttingly*). Huh! I hope I'll be proud of you.

(*The telephone rings.* PATRICIA *starts violently and glances toward the door—then she realizes it is the 'phone and shows signs of great relief.*)

PATRICIA. Oh, I'll answer it.

MRS. HARRINGTON (POP *rising to answer 'phone*). No, I'll answer it.

(POP *crosses on to* C. *to* L.)

(*Into 'phone.*) Hello! Oh, yes. Oh, how do you do, Mrs. Herbert? Which car are you going to catch? The seven-forty? Just a minute. (*Turning to* POP.) What time is it?

POP (*looks at watch*). Seven thirty-two.

MRS. HARRINGTON (*into 'phone*). Yes, I can make the seven-forty. I'll meet you on the car then, and I hope we get a seat. All right. Good-bye. (*Hanging up receiver.*)

POP. You'll have to hurry if you're going to catch the seven-forty. (*Up to* L. *of stairs.*)

MRS. HARRINGTON (*picking up robe from chair* L.C. *Snappishly*). Don't I know it? I know the time. (*She starts for stairs.*) And you'd better find out what she's been up to.

(*Turns and gives* PATRICIA *an angry look, then exits upstairs.*)

POP (*after watching* MRS. HARRINGTON *off, turning and looking searchingly at* PATRICIA). Well, pet—what have you been up to? Are you sure you're not in any trouble, Baby?

PATRICIA. Well, life is like that. One-third of our lives we spend in bed and the other two-thirds in bad!

POP (*coming to* L. *of settee. Shows alarmed worry as he looks at her*). Huh! What do you mean by that, Baby?

PATRICIA. You never have to get out a search warrant to find trouble.

POP (*sits*). What happened?

PATRICIA. Well—— (*Hesitates.*) How much do you love me?

POP (*smiles*). How much do you want?

PATRICIA (*gives a look toward the stairs*). Er—maybe I can tell you about it after a while, Pop.

POP (*nods understandingly*). All right, I got you.

PATRICIA (*brightening*). Have a good trip, Pop?

POP. Grand.

PATRICIA. And were you a good boy? Let me look at your

nose. I can't tell whether that's sunshine or moonshine. (*Kisses* Pop.)

Pop. I swear I never saw a drop of liquor while I was gone.

PATRICIA. That's enough to make anybody swear, isn't it? (*Rising. Pause. Crossing L.*) Still, there's no use of crying over spilt milk, because there's enough water in it already.

Pop. Huh!

(GRACE *enters from stairs. She is now ready to go out. She carries on her arm a rather pretty evening wrap.*)

PATRICIA. Hello, Grace. You going to the Bridge Club with Mother?

GRACE. I'm going out with Billy Caldwell if he ever gets here. He's half an hour late now. (*Puts coat on newel of stairs.*)

PATRICIA (*starts*). Say! You're not going to wear my new wrap, are you?

GRACE. Mother said I could wear it.

PATRICIA. But I haven't worn it myself yet.

GRACE. What difference does that make? You're not going to any special place.

PATRICIA. I'm not going any place in that wrap after you've worn it first!

GRACE (*coming down a step* C.). Mother said I could wear it to-night and if you don't believe me go and ask her yourself.

PATRICIA. Why don't you wear your own wraps?

GRACE. Both of them are soiled. I've got to get them cleaned.

PATRICIA (*very disappointed*). I was saving that wrap for some time when I want to go somewhere all dressed up. Now everybody'll say: "Look! She's wearing her big sister's wrap."

GRACE. You're just flattering yourself. Nobody'll ever take that much notice of you! (*Looks at herself in glass up* R.)

PATRICIA (*with a shrug of resignation*). Well—life is like that. All the world's a stage—but most of us are only stage-hands.

Pop (*who has been sitting with his back to the girls during this, sitting up quickly and looking at her with face wrinkled in curious doubt*). Huh! What do you mean by that, Patricia?

PATRICIA. Oh, I just meant—— Why—oh, well, you mustn't expect everything I say to mean something, Pop. That's being too optimistic.

Pop (*puzzled, looks at her anxiously a moment*). Grace, I don't see why you don't wear your own things. You've got plenty of wraps.

GRACE. I'm engaged to Billy Caldwell. I can't meet the people I have to meet looking like a pauper, can I?

Pop. Oh, I wouldn't say you ever had to look like a pauper.

PATRICIA. Never mind, Pop. It's all right. If it wasn't for the rain there wouldn't be any hay to make when the sun shines.

Pop (*rising quickly—more worried*). Huh!

B

PATRICIA. We all make mistakes, Pop. Remember the time I took a bumble bee for a blackberry ?

POP. Huh !

(*Enter* MRS. HARRINGTON *downstairs. She is now dressed for the street.*)

GRACE (*moving to* L. *and facing up to stairs*). Mother, didn't you say I could wear this wrap ?

MRS. HARRINGTON (*on stairs*). Yes. What about it ?

GRACE. She says I can't wear it.

POP. She didn't say anything of the sort.

MRS. HARRINGTON (*up* C. *Angrily to* POP. *Crosses* C.). Oh, oh ! Now you keep your nose out of this ! (*She turns on* PATRICIA *who is* L.) I said she could wear it to-night—and that's all there is to it. I don't want to hear any more about it. (*Turning away from her.*)

POP. I don't think it's right, May.

MRS. HARRINGTON. You mind your own business.

POP. Well, this is my business.

PATRICIA (*stopping him*). Pop, please—(*crossing up to* C.)—don't say any more. On the subject of business all work and no play makes Jack—— (*Sitting in chair* L.C.)

POP (*again looking at her with the awfully worried look*). Huh ?

MRS. HARRINGTON (*turning at* R.C.). Now I ask you—Is there any sense to that remark ? Is it connected with the conversation in any way ?

POP (*giving* PATRICIA *another worried look and then looking at his watch*). Oh, come on, May, you'd better hurry if you're going to get that car. (*Crossing up to cupboard and taking his hat.*) I'll put you on it.

MRS. HARRINGTON (*sneeringly*). You needn't bother. I can get on the car without any assistance. As long as I have to ride on street-cars like a common washerwoman I can get on myself.

POP (*continues to her and taking her arm*). Aw, come on, May. What's the matter with you ? (*Ad lib. Exit* POP *and* MRS. HARRINGTON *door* R.) You are all the time crying——

(*The moment the door closes after them* PATRICIA'S *whole manner changes as she wheels on* GRACE *and fixes her with a steady, cold look.*)

PATRICIA (L.C.). I've got something to settle with you, young lady !

GRACE. Oh, have you ? (*Coming to* C.)

PATRICIA (*rising*). Where'd you get the money to take Fanny Benson and Hattie McArthur and Jeanne Thompson to the Frontenac for luncheon last Tuesday ?

GRACE (*defiantly*). What business is it of yours where I got the money ?

PATRICIA. It's my business because now I know that you did take that money out of my bureau. I know when you took it and where you spent it.

GRACE (*sitting on the* L. *end of sofa*). Well, what if I did? What are you going to do about it?

PATRICIA. Why didn't you say you took it? Why did you lie about it?

GRACE. Oh, I suppose you're going to tell Father I took it, are you?

PATRICIA (*looks at her coldly*). No. You knew I wouldn't when you took it. That's why you did it.

GRACE. Well, I'll give it back to you when I get it.

PATRICIA. No, you won't. (*Bitterly.*) Everything I've ever had you've taken—and you never gave me back anything. But from now on it's going to be different.

GRACE (*rather ashamed, facing to* R.). Well, I just had to have it—and that's why I took it.

PATRICIA. Do you think Fanny Benson or Hattie McArthur or Jeanne Thompson would steal money to take you to the Frontenac for lunch?

GRACE (*rising*). Don't say I stole it.

PATRICIA. I was just going to say, that trying to be one of the ciphers of the four hundred is ruining you. Your luxuries are becoming too necessary and your necessities are becoming too luxurious.

GRACE. Is that so?

PATRICIA. But I've got to admit one thing: if it wasn't for you our family tree would certainly die.

GRACE. What do you mean by that?

PATRICIA. You're the sap!

GRACE. Oh, shut your big mouth!

PATRICIA. Big mouth! (*Pointing at* GRACE.) That isn't any keyhole in the front of your face either.

GRACE (*enraged*). Just for that I'm glad I took the money!

PATRICIA (*nonchalantly*). Oh, it's all right with me. I wasn't thinking of myself. I was just thinking of you. I'm afraid Billy Caldwell's family might not want him to marry you after they put me in jail.

GRACE (*startled*). What?

PATRICIA. I'm expecting a policeman to knock on the door at any moment.

GRACE (*genuinely alarmed*). My God! What's happened? What have you done now?

PATRICIA. Me? Nothing. You did it.

GRACE (*worried*). What are you talking about?

PATRICIA. I sent away a cheque on the bank and I was going to put that money in the next morning so the cheque would be good. But you stole the money and I couldn't. Now I'm going to get arrested for giving a bad cheque.

GRACE. You're not. That's just a lie. You're just making that up to frighten me.

PATRICIA (*rising*). Am I? (*Taking letter from bosom.*) There's the letter. Read it.

GRACE (*reading and looking at letter again, frightened*). Well, my gracious! How was I to know anything like this was going to happen?

PATRICIA. Your type wouldn't.

GRACE. What? How was I to know?

PATRICIA (*giving her withering look*). You're one of those persons who has to go through the world asking everybody, "What's trumps?"

GRACE. I wish you'd say something once in a while that had some sense to it.

PATRICIA. All right. I'll say something that has sense to it. You'd better get me that money before to-morrow morning, that's all.

GRACE. How can I give you the money? I haven't got it— and I can't get it by to-morrow. I didn't know you wanted that money for anything.

PATRICIA (*looking at her in amazement. Moving up to stairs*). Oh, you didn't? You're always doing things like that. You're always turning the corner in the middle of the block. (*On stairs— starting to go up.*)

GRACE (*crossing up to L. of stairs*). Say, listen, are you going to be home to-night?

PATRICIA (*stops half-way up*). Yes. Why?

GRACE. If Tony Anderson comes, tell him I had an engagement I'd forgotten about and couldn't be here.

(*Start motor effect.*)

PATRICIA. Why didn't you telephone him?

GRACE. Well, I was going to and I forgot.

PATRICIA. Did you invite him here?

GRACE. What is it to you whether I invited him or not?

PATRICIA (*comes back downstairs a step or two*). Do you think that's a nice way to treat Tony Anderson—after all the beautiful things he's done for you—and all the rest of us?

GRACE. He knows I'm engaged to Billy Caldwell—what does he keep hanging around for?

PATRICIA. You could at least feel sorry for him.

(*Stop motor.*)

GRACE. Well, if you feel so sorry for him, why don't you marry him yourself?

PATRICIA. I would in a minute if he ever asked me!

GRACE (*stares in amazement, then laughs*). You don't flatter yourself that he would, do you ?

PATRICIA (*leaning over the banisters—starting to answer her—stopping short*). Well—no—I can't say I do.

GRACE (*laughing*). What a fine chance ! Imagine Tony Anderson asking you to marry him ! Don't be a fool ! (*Sitting on settee.*)

PATRICIA (*smiles*). H'm ! And don't you forget that there's nearly always one more fool in the world than most people think there is.

(*Door-bell rings.*)

(PATRICIA *starts violently with her hand to her heart.*) If that's the police, tell them you did it.

(*Exit* PATRICIA *upstairs quickly.*)

(GRACE *shows a moment's worry, then rather diffidently goes to the door* R. *and opens it.*)

GRACE. Oh ! Hello, Billy !

(*Enter* BILLY CALDWELL *door* R. BILLY *is a handsome, dark-eyed young man, very well dressed in well-tailored evening clothes. He has the air and manner of refinement and wealth. He brings a box containing orchids for* GRACE. *He is very likeable and agreeable, lively, bright, and smiling.*)

BILLY (R.C.). Hello, Grace. Am I on time ?

GRACE (*sweetly*). Yes. I just this moment finished dressing.

BILLY. Here. (*Giving* GRACE *box.*)

GRACE (*opening box*). Oh, Billy ! These are beautiful ! (*Holding up her lips.*)

BILLY (*kissing her*). Glad you like them, dear.

(GRACE *moves up to table above settee and fixes flowers in dress, looking at herself in the glass up* R.)

(BILLY *is sitting on* L. *arm of the settee, facing to* GRACE).

(*Enter* PATRICIA *downstairs.*)

PATRICIA. Hello, Billy.

BILLY. (*Turning to* PATRICIA *and jumping up and shaking hands.*) Hello, Patricia. How are you ?

PATRICIA. Fine, Billy. How are you ?

BILLY. As usual—or better. Aw, say, listen. I'm sorry you can't come to Aunt Jane's little party to-night, Patricia. She was very disappointed when she heard you couldn't come. (*Crosses to couch.*)

PATRICIA (*starting and looking at* GRACE, *then moving to* L.C.). Huh ?

GRACE (*hastily*). Yes, it was too bad; but she'd made a previous engagement she simply couldn't break.

BILLY (*sitting on arm of sofa and facing* L.). Aunt Jane met you once, she tells me. She thinks you're a very sweet little girl.

PATRICIA. Does she? I'm glad. Yes, I remember meeting her at church one night. (*Looking at* GRACE.) Please tell her how sorry I am I couldn't come.

BILLY. I will. Grace, was that your father I saw on the corner?

GRACE. Yes. He got home to-night; so you can meet him.

PATRICIA (*smilingly*). Want me to pray for you, Billy?

BILLY. Sounds like a great idea. I'll probably need a few prayers when he sees me.

PATRICIA (*with a laugh*). Where do you get that stuff?

GRACE. Why, Patricia! Where are you picking up such language? Don't you know that's slang, dear?

PATRICIA. "Where do you get that stuff" isn't slang since Prohibition, is it, Billy?

BILLY (*rising and producing flask*). No. Oh, Patricia, that reminds me, does your father drink anything? (*Handing her flask.*)

PATRICIA. Well, he keeps all the Commandments—but he kinda flops on the Amendments.

GRACE. Patricia! How can you talk like that! Anybody'd think Father was a drinker!

PATRICIA. Oh, I'm just kidding! (*Crossing and placing flask on table above settee.*)

GRACE. I don't see anything funny about it at all!

PATRICIA. Well, life is like that. He who laughs last has just seen the joke. (*Coming* C.) Do you drink, Billy?

BILLY (*sitting on arm of settee and smiling at* GRACE). Well, I've promised to quit entirely as soon as we're married, haven't I, dear? Going to make a sweeping reform.

(*Enter* POP *door* R. BILLY *rises.*)

POP. Oh, hello—— Well——

GRACE (*coming down and meeeting her father* R. *of settee*). This is Billy Caldwell, Father.

POP. Yeah. We know each other to speak. How are you? (*He offers hand. Crossing* GRACE *and meeting* BILLY R.C.)

BILLY (*shakes*). How are you, Mr. Harrington?

POP. Well, I've been hearing some things about you, young man.

BILLY. Hope nobody told you the truth. (*With a laugh.*)

POP (*still shaking his hand*). I'm glad to hear it, my boy. And I think Grace will make you a good little wife.

BILLY (*smiles*). She's promised to make me a good little husband, too.

POP (*laughing, crossing up* L.C. *and hanging up hat*). Well, if she's anything like her mother she probably will.

GRACE (*impatiently*). We'd better be going, Billy. We're late now, aren't we ?

BILLY. Perhaps we'd better. Hate to tear away, Mr. Harrington; but my Aunt Jane is giving a party for Grace to-night—and she's one of those punctual persons.

POP (*coming down again*). That's all right. I'll see you again, son.

BILLY. Yes, I hope we become a lot better acquainted.

POP. Sure. So do I. (*Again they shake hands.*)

BILLY (*going to door with* GRACE, *who opens it*). Good night. Good night, Patricia. (*With a wave of his hand.*)

POP. Good night. Have a good time.

(*Exit* BILLY *and* GRACE.)

PATRICIA (*running down to door*). Oh, Billy,—(*standing in the doorway*)—don't forget to tell your aunt how sorry I am I had a previous engagement, will you ?

BILLY (*off stage*). I won't. Good night.

(*Start motor, which dies away in distance.*)

POP (*c.*). What previous engagement did you have ?

PATRICIA (*closing door and coming slowly to sofa*). None. I didn't know I was invited. Grace must have forgotten to ask me. (*Sadly.*) She's been so busy I guess she forgot it.

POP (*looking at her keenly*). Yeah. That's too bad.

PATRICIA. However, it's just as well. I might have eaten my salad with the wrong soup spoon or something. (*Sitting.*)

POP (*with a smile*). No, you wouldn't. (*Turning away* L.)

PATRICIA. Well—anyway—there's no use crying over spilt milk because there's enough water in it already.

POP (*jumping round*). Huh !

PATRICIA. All the world's a stage—but most of us are only stage-hands.

POP (*starting and looking at her in the greatest alarm and worry*). Huh !—Say—(*coming to her, then hesitating*)—how are you feeling ? (*Sitting by* PATRICIA *on settee on her* L.) Have you had any headaches or anything ? I mean, does your head feel all right ?

PATRICIA (*surprised*). Of course it does. Why ?

POP (*awkwardly*). Why—er—— (*He pauses, unable to frame the words. Then he has a new idea.*) You know, I've been standing out there on the corner thinking about you to-night, Baby.

PATRICIA (*soberly*). Why ?

POP. I never realized it before—but—well—you see—Grace and your mother have the same sort of dispositions—and—well—they get along together—and—it just occurred to me that we're letting you grow up in this house like a perfect stranger. We don't know anything about you. You're just like some unknown person.

PATRICIA (*brightens and smiles*). That sounds funny, doesn't it ?
POP. What ?
PATRICIA. I'm so unknown that even my own father and mother don't know who I am.
POP (*smiles*). It isn't as bad as that, of course. Only—— (*He is at a loss again.*) You know your mother loves you, Baby—— (PATRICIA *shakes her head.*) Yes, she does, Baby. The way she acts—she thinks that's the way to be a good mother, that's all.
PATRICIA (*sadly shaking her head*). Pop, you know I love Ma, don't you ?
POP. Of course you do.
PATRICIA. She won't believe I love her. She thinks I hate her. She thinks I lie awake at night thinking up new ways to get into trouble and make her unhappy.
POP. Aw, she's always thinking things like that. But you do like I do, don't pay any attention, Baby.
PATRICIA (*rising seriously and taking a step back*). If I tell you something, you won't mention it, will you ?
POP. No. What ?
PATRICIA (*kneeling on sofa*). Ma and Aunt Margaret were talking about me the other day and they didn't know I was here.
POP. Yeh !
PATRICIA. Aunt Margaret was sticking up for me and Ma said she didn't want me before I was born—and I've been a curse to her ever since. (*Weeping with her head on the* R. *arm of settee.*)
POP (*trying to pacify her*). Aw, listen, Baby. Your mother's always saying things she don't mean at all. You know, she ain't herself. She nearly died when you were born and she's been nervous and hysterical ever since. But she does love you. She'd die if anything ever happened to you. And even if she didn't want you, Baby, I want you. (*She sits up sidewise to him looking away.*) Why, listen, Pat—I'd go to hell for you. (*He pauses.*) I mean before my time.

(PATRICIA *looks up suddenly. The comedy of his remark strikes, making her give a broad smile. She looks at him again with the smile—and then, kindness and love do to her what unfairness couldn't —she suddenly wilts and starts to cry, silently but furiously, with shaking shoulders. She goes to him and falls in his lap—crying. POP, for several moments, clumsily patting her shoulders and unable to find something to say.*)

(*Toying with a lock of her hair which he curls up and uncurls.*) You haven't been very happy in this house, kiddie—but from now on it's going to be different. You're going to forget. I'm your old man and we're just going to be a couple of pals, huh ? Ain't we ?
PATRICIA (*still crying, now turns and faces him in his arms and putting her arms around him, clings to him*). Uh-huh !
POP. And whenever you're worried and unhappy and get so

miserable you talk kinda queer you're coming right to your old man and talk it all over, ain't you?

PATRICIA (*looks up at him suddenly*). Huh?

POP (*sitting back and patting her shoulder*). You're in some kinda trouble now, Baby. And you're going to tell me, ain't you? And I won't scold you—no matter what it is. Is it about some man?

PATRICIA (*shaking her head*). Huh-uh.

POP. Come on, tell your old man what it is, Baby.

PATRICIA (*turning and bracing herself*). Well—er—there's some books advertised in all the magazines. And you send three dollars— and then they send you the books—and then you send them the rest of the money.

POP. And you want them, huh?

PATRICIA. No. I got them. And, Pop—you know that money Uncle Mack gave me for my birthday—and the money you gave me when you went away?

POP. Yeah?

PATRICIA. Well, I sent a cheque on the Savings Bank—and then I was going to put the money in the bank so the cheque would be good—and—and—I lost it. (*Facing out in front.*)

POP. Where?

PATRICIA (*shaking her head*). I don't know. I just lost it some- where—all of it. And now they're going to do something to me for giving a bad cheque.

POP. Who?

PATRICIA (*giving him the letter.*) Look!

POP (*reading it. Rising and crossing to* L.C.). I'd like to see them do it. (*He produces his wallet.*) Here.

(PATRICIA *crosses to him.*)

Send them their old twelve dollars. And here's a couple for your- self. (*Giving her money and putting away wallet and letter in his pocket.*) Now—does that fix it?

PATRICIA (*kissing him*). Pop, you just saved my life, that's all!

POP. What the devil do you want with books? What kind of books?

PATRICIA (*sitting on chair* L.C., *looking away*). I don't want to tell you, Pop.

POP. I won't scold you, Baby.

PATRICIA. That ain't what I'm afraid of. You'll laugh at me.

POP (*shaking his head*). No, I won't. I promise you I won't laugh. What kind of books?

PATRICIA (*rising and crossing, sitting on* R. *of sofa. With an effort*). Well,—when a fellow isn't as beautiful as her big sister— and she hasn't got very swell clothes—well—(*she hesitates, looking at* POP)—well—you've got to do something! Isn't that right?

POP (L.C., *puzzled*). Huh?

PATRICIA. I mean, if you're not ravishingly beautiful you've got to be at least—well—brilliant and witty—and everything. Haven't you ?

Pop. Huh !

Patricia (*she thinks as she talks, obviously recalling words of some formal statement she tries to remember*). I mean—and you want to be welcomed everywhere—and be the life of the party—and be adored for your brilliance and wit—and be the most popular girl— (*she stops, stuck, looking up at* Pop)—well, you've got to do that, haven't you ?

Pop. I don't get you, Baby.

Patricia. Well, the books are called " Wise and Witty Sayings for All Occasions." (*Pause.*)

Pop. Yeh ?

Patricia. You memorize all the jokes and everything—and then when anybody says anything—you give them repartee.

Pop (*a wide, relieved smile comes over his face*). When did you get these books ?

Patricia. There's a set of four of them. I got them two weeks ago.

Pop (*suddenly breaks into hearty laughter. It tickles him immensely. He enjoys it a long time*). This is rich.

Patricia (*disappointed*). You said you wouldn't laugh.

Pop. Listen, Baby. I'm not laughing at you. I'm laughing at a good joke.

Patricia. Yes, and I'm it.

Pop (R.C.). No. Wait till I tell you. You've been trying these wise and witty sayings on your mother, haven't you ?

Patricia. Yes.

Pop. Well, when I came home to-night she said you were saying such queer things that she thought you were going out of your mind.

Patricia. Did she ? I didn't have anybody else to practise on. I just wanted to see how they went.

Pop. Where are these books ? Can I see them ?

Patricia (*beckoning to* Pop, *who crosses and sits beside her on settee. Playfully putting his hand over his eyes,* Pop *looking through his fingers. She gets books from under cushions of settee*). Ready ? Look. Here's the advertisement that made me buy them. (*Handing it to him.*)

Pop (*reading*). " Do you wish to be the life of the party ? Do you long to be popular ? Do you want to be lionized by the ladies ? Do you want the men to adore you for your wit and brilliance ? " (*Puts on his glasses. Reads the ad. with an amused smile.*) " Repartee is only repertoire." (*He laughs.*) " Memorize them and have them ready." (*He laughs again.*)

Patricia (*kneeling up on sofa*). Here, Pop. (*Handing him a book.*)

Pop. Do they tell you how to work it ?

Patricia (*excitedly*). Uh-huh. For instance ; You go to an

hotel and ask the clerk for a room.   He says : " Have you got a
reservation ? "   And then you say : " What do you take me for—
an Indian ? "

Pop (laughing).   These might be a good thing for me, huh ?

Patricia.   Uh-huh.   And they increase your vocabulary five
thousand words.

Pop.   Say !   (Looking round at stairs.)   Don't let your mother
get a-hold of these.

Patricia.   Nobody knows I've got them, only you—and don't
you tell.

Pop.   Why does a chicken——   Shucks !   These ain't nothing
but old jokes.   You got stung.   They're not worth the money.

Patricia (rising, disappointed).   Aren't they, Pa ?

Pop.   No !

Patricia.   Oh, gee !   (Sitting again.)

Pop (a light dawns on him, puts book on sofa—to be played with
later).   What's the matter, Baby ?   Don't the boys pay you enough
attention ?

Patricia.   Huh ?   (She looks at him—at a loss.)

Pop.   Your Ma and I was talking about it to-night.   Don't none
of the boys ever ask you to go out with them ?

Patricia (sitting up).   Huh !   Lots of them do—only——

Pop.   Only what ?

Patricia.   Only the right one.

Pop (interested).   Oh !   Is there one of them you kinda like ?

Patricia.   Kinda like !   Huh !   Gosh !

Pop.   You mean you like him a lot ?

Patricia (rising).   Like him !   Gee !

Pop.   Who is he ?   Do I know him ?

Patricia.   You'd think I was crazy if I told you.

Pop.   No, I wouldn't.   Who ?

Patricia.   Well, it's Tony.

Pop (surprised).   Tony !   Tony Anderson ?

Patricia (looking down shamefaced).   Uh-huh.

Pop.   Yeh !   How long have you liked him ?

Patricia.   Ever since the first time I saw him.

Pop.   Well—does he like you ?

Patricia (sadly).   He doesn't even know I'm alive.

Pop.   Huh ?   (Sitting back in the settee laughing.)

Patricia (kneeling on couch).   Oh, he's wonderful to me—but
he's wonderful to everybody.   Only he's always been so much in
love with Grace—he hardly knows there is such a person as me.
I'm just the same to him as a piece of furniture or something.

Pop (taking her hand).   Are you sure you love him ?

Patricia (shows by little uneven pats of her hand for heart-beats).
Of course.   If you don't know whether you're in love or not—
that's a sign you're not ; because love is like a toothache—when
you've got it nobody has to tell you.

POP (*laughs, then suddenly asks*). Is that one of those jokes out of the book?

PATRICIA. Yes. See, that worked in pretty good, didn't it? (*With a smile.*)

POP (*thinking*). Well, now that Grace is going to marry Billy Caldwell, I don't see any reason why you shouldn't marry Tony.

PATRICIA (*eagerly*). Don't you, Pop?

POP. No. Besides, I think you'd make Tony a wonderful little wife.

PATRICIA (*earnestly*). Do you, Pop?

POP. Sure I do. And listen, maybe I can figure out some way to sort of help you to get him.

PATRICIA. Oh, gee, Pop! That would be wonderful!

POP. Now, listen, I think——

(*The door-bell rings.*)

Who's that?

PATRICIA (*excitedly jumping up and moving up to the stairs*). Maybe it's Tony. He's coming up to-night to see Grace.

POP (*winks*). Yeh, well, if it is, just watch me fix something. (*He goes to door and opens it.*)

(*Enter* TONY ANDERSON *door* R. TONY *is a blue-eyed young man of about 25, blond, very handsome, and very well-dressed. He conveys the idea of wealth and taste—but, although very pleasant and agreeable in manner he is rather shy and quiet, almost timid.*)

(*Breezily.*) Hello, Tony—— (*They shake hands heartily.*)

TONY. Hello, Mr. Harrington.

POP. How are you?

TONY. I'm fine, thanks.

POP. Glad to see you.

TONY (*crosses to* C.). Hello, Patricia.

PATRICIA. Hello, Tony (*meeting him and ready to shake hands.* TONY *handing her his hat and turning back to* POP). (*Sadly looking at hat and then at* TONY.) I'll take your hat. (*Taking hat up to arm-chair* L. *of stairs.*)

TONY (C.). Thanks.

POP (*on* TONY'S R.). How's the real estate business, Tony?

TONY. Very good, thanks.

POP. That's good—glad to hear it.

TONY. Oh, say, I'm opening up a new development next week. Want to make a little piece of quick money?

POP (*smiles*). Sure I would.

TONY. Come in Monday and I'll show you some lots you can turn over quickly.

POP. That sounds great. But listen, don't say anything to anybody about me fooling with lots. I bought some lots in Florida once and lost two hundred dollars on each lot. Mrs. Harrington raised the devil.

Tony (*with a smile*). Did she ? What'd she say ?

Pop. Can't tell you exactly—because she hasn't finished talking about it yet.

Tony (*laughing heartily*). What did you buy ?—beach lots ?

Pop. Yep. I bit. And I got a mouthful.

Patricia. Uh-huh. At low tide the ocean was at the bottom of the lots—and at high tide the lots were at the bottom of the ocean. (*All laugh.*)

Pop (*moving up to staircase*). Well—I'll drop in Monday, Tony. I know anything you sell me will be O.K.

Tony. Thanks. Tell Grace I'm here, will you ?

Pop. Oh—er——

Patricia. Oh, dear, Tony—didn't Grace get you ? She was trying all day. She called you up half a dozen times to tell you she found she had made a previous engagement.

Tony (*blankly*). Isn't she here ?

Patricia. Oh, she'll feel terrible, Tony.

Tony. Oh, that's all right. (*Moving up as if to get his hat.*)

Pop (*coming down a step R.C.*). Don't go on that account, Tony.

Tony. Well, I'll tell you—(*looking at watch*)—I had a business appointment——

Pop. Wait a minute, Tony. You've got me worried. You're working too hard. Now you mustn't do that, Tony. You want to take it easy once in a while. Take a little time off, and relax——

Tony (*looking at* Pop, *surprised*). Huh ?

Pop. Yes, sir. You ought to take an hour off—in the evening—and just forget all about business.

Tony. Yes, I guess I have been working pretty hard.

Pop. You bet you have. Sit down here and talk to this youngster a while—she was just complaining that she was lonesome—and it'll do you both good. Yes, sir !

Tony (*sitting on settee*). Well, maybe I can stay a little while.

Pop. That's the stuff. Have a cigar. Make yourself at home. See you Monday, Tony.

Tony. All right. Good night, Mr. Harrington.

Patricia. Good night, Pop.

(Pop *goes off with a funny expression. He lingers a moment to motion to* Patricia *to go after* Tony. *Exit* Pop *upstairs.*)

(*Crosses to* Tony.) That's lovely of you to show Pop how to make some money, Tony—but you're always doing wonderful things for people.

Tony (*smiling and shrugging his shoulders*). Well, I haven't anybody of my own to do things for. (*Looking at her and smiling meaningly.*) I'm not the lucky sort, I guess.

PATRICIA (*smiling*). Life is like that. All the world's a stage—but most of us are only stage-hands.

TONY (*smiling at* PATRICIA). That's right.

PATRICIA (*behind chair* L.C.). But you must look on the bright side of things, Tony. When your feet get tired walking—always remember what a fine, cheap ride the rest of you is getting for nothing.

TONY (*sitting back in settee and laughing*). You're a philosopher!

PATRICIA (*pleased with herself*). And remember—if it wasn't for the rain there wouldn't be any hay to make when the sun shines.

TONY. I wish I could think of clever things like that to say. I always think of the clever thing I should have said a couple of days later.

PATRICIA (*with a smile*). I used to be like that myself. (*Crosses to table above* TONY.)

TONY (*looking round*). Your father said you were lonesome. What are you lonesome about?

PATRICIA. Oh—I don't know. Don't you ever get lonesome?

TONY. Lonesome! I'm beginning to think I have a lonesome complex.

PATRICIA. Have you, Tony?

TONY (*shrugs*). Well, you know—no father or mother I can remember—raised by a lot of trustees and nurses and executors—it sort of starts you off lonesome.

PATRICIA (*coming down on* L. *of settee*). I must have a lonesome complex, too—I'm lonesome all the time. (*She suddenly brightens.*) But life is just like a golf game—if four play it's a foursome—if two play it's a twosome—and when you play alone—it's a lonesome.

TONY (*rising—amused*). That's good. Say, you and I ought to start a lonesome club.

PATRICIA (*smiling*). Maybe we should.

TONY (*with a smile*). Might be a great idea. I know a fellow who has a girl friend—they're not in love with each other—just friends, you know—and he tells her all his troubles and she tells him her troubles. They call it the Lonesome Club.

PATRICIA (*sitting chair* L.C.—*eagerly*). What a perfectly marvellous idea! It would be wonderful to have some fellow you could really talk to.

TONY (*smiles*). Would I do?

PATRICIA (*smiles*). Would I do?

TONY (*sticks out his hand*). Shake!

(*Both shake.*)

(TONY *crosses up and brings chair from up* R. *to on her* R.)

PATRICIA. Right!

TONY (*sitting on chair facing to* PATRICIA). Only trouble with this club is that you know all my troubles.

PATRICIA (*sympathetically*). Yes, and I know how to sympathize with you, too.

TONY (*amazed*). You do? Have you been in love?

PATRICIA (*turning her chair facing him*). Always—er—I mean—constantly—er—that is—frequently.

TONY (*amazed*). And was it unlucky?

PATRICIA. Worse than that—it is unlucky.

TONY. You mean you're in love with somebody now?

PATRICIA (*frightened—hesitating and turning her head away*). Uh-huh.

TONY (*looking at her a moment*). Do you know—I'm glad I came over here to-night. Everybody laughs at my theories—but I'd like to try an experiment, Patricia.

PATRICIA (*startled*). With me?

TONY. Yes. Would you let me?

PATRICIA (*swallows and then takes the brave course*). Well, America's the place where they try everything once but the criminals!

TONY (*delighted*). You mean you will?

PATRICIA (*flustered a bit. She sort of edges her chair a little nearer to his*). Well, what do you want to do?

TONY. I'll show you how to get this fellow you're in love with.

PATRICIA (*open-mouthed with astonishment*). What's that?

TONY. I know it sounds foolish, Patricia, but listen to reason. When people want to learn how to play bridge they take bridge lessons—when they want to learn how to play golf, they take golf lessons—but in the most important game in the whole world they think they can play any old way—without knowing anything. That's why there's so many unhappy love affairs.

PATRICIA (*round-eyed*). You mean you're going to give me Love Lessons?

TONY. Why not? Knowledge is Power. (*Rising and crossing down, sitting on L. of sofa—finds himself sitting on PATRICIA'S book ; without examining it he holds it in his hands.*)

PATRICIA. Gosh! I always thought husbands were like the measles—you catch them or you don't catch them.

TONY (*laughing heartily*). That's witty, Patricia. You ought to write all those things down and put them in a book. (*Is about to open the book.*)

PATRICIA (*crossing quickly to him and taking book from him and placing under cushion, laughing awkwardly*). Yeh! You don't want to hold that! What were you saying? (*Sitting on settee R. of TONY.*)

TONY. Let me try this experiment, will you? I want to see if I'm right.

PATRICIA (*hesitatingly—placing the cushion between them*). Well —er—do you think it would be right for me to get him that way —I mean—would it be sportsmanlike?

TONY. Why not? "All's fair in love and war," isn't it?

PATRICIA (*confused and frightened at the swift happenings. Looks round at book*). Gracious! I don't know what to say now! (*Rising and crossing* L.C.)

TONY (*rising*). Please let me try it, Patricia. I have a theory that any ordinarily good-looking girl could win any man she wanted if she did the right things. Please.

PATRICIA (*hesitates. Turning to him*). Well—but listen, Tony—if anything happens—I mean if it turns out all wrong—you'll remember you're the one who wanted to do it, won't you?

TONY (*up* R.C.). It isn't going to turn out wrong. I'm positive—because I'm able to analyse myself. And any man who can analyse himself and knows himself knows ninety per cent. about every other man. Will you do it?

PATRICIA (*struggles—sighs with worry*). Well——

TONY (*turning away*). Well, of course if you don't want to——

PATRICIA. Yes—well—yes.

TONY (*turning again quickly*). Oh, that's great! I never thought I was going to have a chance to try this experiment.

PATRICIA. What do you want me to do? (*Eagerly.*)

TONY. Well—the first thing is to be sure you love him.

PATRICIA. Oh, I know I love him.

TONY. And you really want to marry him,—do you?

PATRICIA. Do I? If he ever says "Wilt thou?" to me—I'm going to wilt.

TONY. How long have you loved him?

PATRICIA. Ever since the first time I saw him——

TONY. Does he love you? I mean—does he know you love him?

PATRICIA. He doesn't dream. The first time he saw me I was just a kid—and I'm still a kid to him, I guess. He doesn't even know I'm grown up.

TONY (*thoughtfully*). Uh-huh. Well—what are your reactions toward him? What makes you know that you love him?

PATRICIA. Well—whenever I want to get a thrill I just go and look at his house and my heart goes—— (*She illustrates with quick little pats over her heart.*)

TONY. Uh-huh! (*Nodding his head.*) Those are the symptoms—I don't want you to make a mistake. I want you to be sure you love him—because getting him is so simple.

PATRICIA. Is it?

TONY. Yes. By the way, who is he?

PATRICIA. What's that?

TONY. Who is he?

PATRICIA (*flabbergasted*). Oh!—Why—er—— (*She laughs.*) You'd be surprised.

TONY (*smiles*). Oh, I can guess who it is. I've seen you dining with him a couple of times lately.

PATRICIA. Who?

TONY. Mr. O'Flaherty. (*Smilingly.*) He's sort of old, isn't he?

PATRICIA (*hastily*). Oh, it isn't him.

TONY (*suddenly*). If my theory is right, it doesn't make any difference who it is. Never mind telling me. I don't have to know that.

PATRICIA (*very pleased*). What's the first thing I do?

TONY. The first and most important thing to remember is: Don't you wait for him to come after you. You go after him.

PATRICIA. What?

TONY. The woman always does the love-making.

PATRICIA. Oh, you can't mean that!

TONY. Always. Oh, I don't mean she runs after him and says: "I love you. Marry me." She doesn't have to. She's too smart. She does the love-making—but she makes the man think he's doing it. See? On the subject of love a woman is always fifty times smarter than a man.

PATRICIA (*with a smile*). Now, Tony, don't condemn us with faint praise!

TONY. I mean it. She is. Now, the first thing she does is to make the man interested in her.

PATRICIA (*with a gasp of astonishment*). How?

TONY. By being interested in him.

PATRICIA. I've been interested in him since I was a little girl and it hasn't done the least bit of good.

TONY. Ah! But you weren't interested in the right way. Let me show you. Every man carries around in the back of his head some little pet dream, or hope, or ambition. You find out what it is and be interested in helping him to realize it. When he finds you're interested in that, he'll begin to be interested in you.

PATRICIA (*puzzled*). Huh?

TONY (*positively*). Sure! Men are always interested in people who are taking a lot of interest in them.

PATRICIA. How will I find out what his little pet dream is?

TONY. Ah! That's where you have got to be clever. You've got to find that out yourself. But it isn't hard. Men love to talk about themselves. Lead him on. Ask him questions—he'll never suspect—he'll be too dumb.

PATRICIA (*thinking*). I've got to find that out myself, huh? (*Rising.*)

TONY. Yes. I can't help you on that. That's your job.

PATRICIA (*with sudden flash of hope*). Wait a minute—I'm not sure what you mean—what is your little pet dream, Tony—so I'll know what to look for?

TONY (*thinking a minute*). Oh—mine's too silly. (*Almost rising.*)

PATRICIA (*sitting on arm of chair* L.C., *eagerly*). I won't laugh at it. Please tell me yours, Tony—so I'll know what to look for? I won't laugh. (*Sitting on chair.*)

Tony (*looking at her*). This is funny. I never had the nerve to tell it to anyone before. (*Cheerfully.*) That's the great thing about having some disinterested girl friend to talk to, isn't it ?

Patricia (*placing her hand on his knee*). Please tell me, Tony ?

Tony. Well, you know that place of mine out at Lake Como ?

Patricia. Yes.

Tony. It's a pretty little place inside. My father built it for my mother for a summer place, they tell me. Well—I dream about it all covered with pretty vines and window-boxes with flowers. And me married to some sweet little girl who loves me—you know —not because I've got a lot of property—but just for myself.

Patricia (*eagerly*). Uh-huh.

Tony. And there's a peach of a breakfast-room out there. And I always dream about her sitting across the breakfast table from me in the morning—pouring my coffee. (*Looking straight out in front, Patricia following his gaze, then looking at her and laughing.*) That's silly enough, isn't it ?

Patricia (*stares straight out a moment soberly as though visualizing the picture*). I think that's beautiful ! It's just—beautiful, Tony.

Tony (*pleased*). It is, isn't it ?

(*A pause.*)

Patricia (*coming out of her trance with almost a sigh*). What's the next thing I do ?

Tony (*thinking*). Well, I'd manage some scheme to see him as often as possible. That's something else you'll have to figure out for yourself.

Patricia (*eagerly*). Uh-huh. (*Thinking.*) But listen, Tony— all this is, you know, sort of new and hard to understand. You'll have to come over and talk to me a lot before I'll understand it like you do. But I suppose you're too busy, aren't you ?

Tony (*eagerly*). No ! I'd love to !

Patricia (*anxiously*). That's wonderful. You'll never know what you're doing for me, Tony ! What's the next thing I do ?

Tony (*looking at watch and rising*). Well, that's about enough for a beginning—— (*Placing chair up stage.*) Oh, say, there is one thing that's very important. It's the truth—and every married woman knows it. It's the principal thing ! (*Returning to her.*)

Patricia (*eagerly*). What ?

Tony. The thing which an average man cannot get along without is an audience.

Patricia (*amazed*). An audience ?

Tony. An audience. It isn't any fun when a man puts over a big business deal, or gets his salary raised, or wins something, unless he has somebody he can go and tell it to—somebody who pats him on the back and tells him how clever he was.

Patricia (*absorbing it all in*). Uh-huh.

Tony. In other words—give him a lot of applause. (Patricia

nods.) He's very vain and he needs it. Be his cheer leader. Give him more cheers than he gets anywhere else and you'll notice him beginning to hang around you. I've got to skip now, Patricia. (*Going up for his hat.* PATRICIA *rises and follows him up* C.) Say, this fellow isn't in love with anybody else, is he?

PATRICIA (*sadly*). Yes, that's the worst of it. He loves somebody else.

TONY (*disappointed*). Oh, that's too bad! Does she love him?

PATRICIA. No. (*Shaking her head and looking up at* TONY.) She's going to marry somebody else and he's broken-hearted over it.

TONY (*suddenly, moving down stage*). Great! Great! This is the psychological moment. That's the time to get them—on the rebound!

PATRICIA. Is it? (*Following him to* R.C.)

TONY. Sure! Go after him, Patricia. He's probably some poor sap—wandering around hoping somebody will love him! Just like I am.

PATRICIA (*very softly*). Are you that way, Tony?

TONY. I'm worse, really. I know I'm a darned fool—but I don't suppose I'll ever get over loving Grace.

PATRICIA (*with a sigh*). Oh, I hope so, Tony.

TONY (*holding out his hand*). Whoever this chap is he's a lucky dog, Patricia—to have a girl like you in love with him. (*He looks at her a moment.*) Isn't it funny? (*Looking keenly in her face and smiling.*) This is the first time you and I ever really got acquainted, isn't it?

PATRICIA (*nodding her head*). That's right!

TONY. Well, I've got to get along. (*Crossing to door* R. *and opening it, facing door and not turning.*) Oh, what are you doing Monday night? Maybe I'll come over and have another talk with you.

PATRICIA. Please do, Tony.

TONY. By that time you'll have some progress to report. (*Turning to her.*) And cheer up, Patricia. (*Crossing back to her.*) Whoever this fellow is, if my theory works out right you're going to get him. (*His hands on her shoulders, she looking up in his face.*)

PATRICIA. I hope you're right.

TONY (*taking her hand*). Good night, Patricia.

PATRICIA. Good night!

(TONY *almost kisses her, then changes his mind and kisses her hand —exits, shutting the door as he goes.*)

(*Looking after him without moving, holding her hand in the position he left it when he kissed it.*) Isn't that a hell of a place to kiss a person?

CURTAIN.

Time of representation : 60 minutes.

ACT II

NOTE.—*Place book under seat on divan.*

At rise.—MRS. HARRINGTON *and* POP *are discovered.* MRS. HARRINGTON *is sitting on the sofa.* POP *sits* L.C. MRS. HARRINGTON *is sobbing into her handkerchief and* POP *sits in a slump, gloomily looking straight out front.* MRS. HARRINGTON *is dressed as though to go out without her wrap.* POP *wears his street clothes.*

POP (*gloomily*). Oh, well—there's no use feeling so bad about it. It isn't as bad as if she'd committed a murder or something.

MRS. HARRINGTON. Don't start to defend her. I'll never be able to look anybody in the face again.

POP. Oh, bosh!

MRS. HARRINGTON (*crying*). Yes—bosh! This is what you get for bringing her up the way you have. Now she's disgraced us before the whole town.

POP (*tartly*). Oh, write that on a cake of ice.

(GRACE *enters from street door* R. *Slams door. She is in evening clothes and wrap—all ready to go out—and she carries in her hand a newspaper.*)

MRS. HARRINGTON. Don't slam that door.

GRACE (*angrily, coming below settee and holding out paper*). There! Look at it! I told you it was in the paper! .She took our paper away with her so you wouldn't see it. It's in both the papers. Read it!

POP (*takes paper from her*). Where is it?

(MRS. HARRINGTON *makes a groan.*)

GRACE (*angrily snatching paper, turning page, and pointing as she gives it back*). There it is—for the whole town to read. There's your sweet little daughter Patricia. (*Puts hat up in cupboard.*)

POP (*reading headlines*). "Patricia Harrington returns Eisenwein trophy. She admits she won by cheating."

MRS. HARRINGTON. I wouldn't be a bit surprised if she did it on purpose. (*Wails.*) She said she was going to get her name in the paper—there it is. I hope you're proud of her!

POP (*looking up from paper*). I don't see why they had to put

36

this in the paper. It's a damned outrage! (*Putting paper on chair up stage.*)

GRACE (*up* L.C.). Oh, that's right! Blame it on the paper instead of her. She's the one that cheated to win the cup, isn't she?

MRS. HARRINGTON. As long as she had to practically steal the cup, why didn't she keep her mouth shut about it? But no—she'd have to go and tell everybody she stole it and disgrace the whole family.

POP (*moving to* L., *worried*). Well, she probably thought she was doing the right thing.

GRACE (*crossing to chair* L.C.). What will the Caldwells think! That's another thing!

POP. They probably won't think anything!

GRACE. Well, they're not the sort who associate with the kind of people who get their names in the papers. You know very well what they'll think. (*Turning up stage to stairs.*)

MRS. HARRINGTON (*wailing*). I don't see why Mr. Eisenwein has to go around offering silver cups—anyway. Why doesn't he attend to his department store and mind his own business?

POP (*impatiently*). Oh, dry up! There's no use crying over spilt milk. (*Turning as though to read the paper again when he gets a bright idea.*) Because there's enough water in it already!

MRS. HARRINGTON (*emitting a startled scream, wrinkles her face in a contortion and hysterically holds her hands over her ears*). Oh!

(POP *and* GRACE *start and stare at her astounded.*)

If anybody mentions spilt milk again in this house I'll shriek!

POP (*glaring at her. Crosses*). Listen here, May, it seems to me we're doing a lot of worrying on the wrong end of this thing. Instead of wondering what people are going to think—we ought to be wondering what's happened to Pat. God knows what she's liable to do with all this darned nonsense in the papers.

GRACE. I, for one, don't care what she does!

POP (*up* C.). You're her sister and you ought to care.

GRACE. Well, I don't. So there!

POP. Maybe you'd change your mind if she's gone away somewhere and killed herself over this.

GRACE. You know better than that. She'll come sneaking back here and try to explain that she thought it was "the sportsmanlike thing to do"—and then you'll forgive her.

POP. That's probably just exactly why she did do it.

GRACE (*turning to her mother and sitting* L.C.). There you are! He's forgiven her already! Did you hear that?

MRS. HARRINGTON (*wails*). That's what you get for letting her join the Country Club. I told you not to!

GRACE. Yes, and I told you she'd do something out there that would make everybody think we're a lot of nobodies. And now she's done it.

POP (*turning*). That ain't so——

MRS. HARRINGTON. Ain't! Oh!

GRACE. What she did was an insult to every woman in the Country Club who was trying to win that cup. Our family will be very popular with them after this!

POP (*worried*). Where do you suppose she could be?

GRACE. I don't care where she is! I could almost wish I'd never see her again.

POP (*angrily*). You stop talking like that—it's unlucky. You might get your wish. (*Moving down* L.)

GRACE. No such luck!

POP (*stopping, turning and glaring at her incredulously*). You're the queerest sister I ever saw!

GRACE. Well, the question is—what are you going to do about it when she gets here?

POP. What am I supposed to do?

GRACE. I'd know what to do if I was her father—I tell you that! I'd teach her to act like a regular little crook!

POP (*glaring at her*). Yes, I suppose you would. (*To* MRS. HARRINGTON.) Was Pat here when the paper came to-night?

MRS. HARRINGTON (*still seated on sofa*). Yes. The door-bell rang and she went to answer it and it was the evening paper. The next thing I knew she had put on her hat and was gone.

POP (C., *picking up paper*). She probably saw that stuff in the paper and was afraid to stay here. (*He paces about a little and again looks at his watch.*) I wish I knew where she was!

(*There is a timid little knock at the door. At this there is a bracing up and stiffening movement from* GRACE *and* MRS. HARRINGTON. *The door opens. Enter* PATRICIA *door* R. *She opens the door a little, looks in all smiles, trying desperately to make the thing a humorous matter—and slowly comes in. She closes the door behind her, stands with her back to it a moment and waits as they all, including* POP, *watch her in stony silence.*)

PATRICIA. Hello.

GRACE. Oh, you're here, are you? (*She braces herself for the row.*)

PATRICIA (*staring a moment*). I'll bet you wouldn't believe me if I said " no." (*There is no response from any of the three. After a moment she speaks again.*) Aren't any of you even speaking to me? (*There is another stony silence.*) Gosh! It seems good to see the old place again!

POP (*sternly*). Where have you been, Patricia? .

PATRICIA. I ran away!

POP. Huh?

PATRICIA (*hastily*). But I came back—and—and—well—(*making a gesture of what-does-it-matter*)—here I am or there you are—or whatever's going to happen!

Pop (*looking at her keenly*). You ran away ?

PATRICIA. Yes, Pop. But I thought it over, and I decided the sportsmanlike thing to do was to come back and face the music—so—(*smiling ingratiatingly at* Pop)—you may fire when ready, Gridley—and the Lord help me and do it darned quick !

MRS. HARRINGTON (*glaring*). I suppose you're very proud of yourself, aren't you ?

GRACE (*venomously*). What are the Caldwells going to think of us now ? (*Glaring at* PATRICIA *with utter hate.*)

PATRICIA. I don't care what the Caldwells think——

GRACE (*giving her an angry look*). Oh, you don't care what they think ?

PATRICIA. Please don't look at me like that, Grace ! I didn't know this was going to happen !

GRACE (*savagely*). I'll look at you any way I please.

PATRICIA. You're very generous, aren't you ? You'd give a fellow the last dirty look you've got !

MRS. HARRINGTON (*furiously*). Uh, uh, uh, you stop talking like that and tell us why you did it ! You've disgraced us before the whole town !

GRACE. Members of the Country Club are supposed to be ladies and gentlemen—not cheats and crooks ! (*Rising and moving up* c.)

(POP *crosses to* L.)

Pop. Wait a minute, Grace. Don't be so quick calling people crooks around here.

MRS. HARRINGTON (*angrily*). Well, what else was it ?

PATRICIA. Maybe it was crooked—but it was intelligent !

GRACE (*in an attitude of despair*). Intelligent ! Oh, my heavens !

(PATRICIA *stares at her.*)

MRS. HARRINGTON (*furious*). Why did you do it ?

PATRICIA (*heaves a deep sigh*). Well—I'll tell you how it was.

GRACE. That's right. Explain it away. I suppose it's a mere nothing !

PATRICIA. I don't have to say anything—but you're all related to me—and I'm—well—I'm sorry I got my name in the papers. I didn't think they'd publish it.

MRS. HARRINGTON. You know better than that. You told us last week you'd have your name in the papers and we'd all be proud of you !

PATRICIA (*moving to below settee*). I thought it was going to be something you would be proud of.

GRACE (*above settee* R.C., *sarcastically*). We are—very !

PATRICIA (*beginning to look beaten and hopeless. Turning to* Pop). If you'd let me explain it——

Pop. What the devil did you do it for, Pat ? You had a high

school education and you used to go to Sunday School when you was little. Didn't you know no better ?

PATRICIA (*hurt, looks at him*). Gee ! Pop, it was the only sportsmanlike thing to do. I wouldn't have come back only I thought maybe you'd listen to me and understand it——

POP (*coming to himself, facing away from her to* L.). Why, I'm going to listen ! Go right ahead and explain it. (*Turning to his wife and* GRACE, *with great authority.*) And you two keep still while she's doing it. We've had enough howling and bawling around here about it to-night. Now shut up and listen to what she's got to say. Go on, Pat.

PATRICIA (*addressing herself to* POP. *Crosses to* C.). Well—(*she heaves a heavy sigh*)—when Mr. Eisenwein offered the silver cup I went around and asked who was going to decide the contest.

POP. Yes.

PATRICIA (*pleadingly to* POP). That was all right so far, wasn't it ? There was nothing wrong with that, was there ?

POP (*positively*). Of course not ! (*To* GRACE *and* MRS. HARRINGTON.) What was wrong with that ?

GRACE. Of course not !

(PATRICIA *turns on her angrily.*)

PATRICIA (*pulling herself up and sighing heavily*). Well—I found out that Mr. Eisenwein was going to decide who was right himself, and it occurred to me that it didn't make any difference how right anybody was unless they picked out the three Americans Mr. Eisenwein thought were the ones. Now was there anything wrong with that ?

POP. No. What was wrong with that ? (*To* MRS. HARRINGTON *and* GRACE.) There you are ! She's able to explain it !

MRS. HARRINGTON (*to end of sofa*). I'm waiting to hear why you stole that cup.

PATRICIA (*heaves another sigh*). Well—you know that big, fat Mr. O'Flaherty, of Rosenbloom and O'Flaherty ?

POP. Yes ?

PATRICIA. Well—he and Mr. Eisenwein are always together— you know, they go around together—and I found out Mr. O'Flaherty didn't know anything about Mr. Eisenwein offering the silver cup——

POP (*looks at her keenly*). Yes. Uh-huh.

PATRICIA. And Mr. O'Flaherty asked me if I'd go to dinner with him some time——

POP (*sternly*). Oh, I see.

PATRICIA (*hastily*). But he's an awfully nice man, Pop. He's a gentleman—he's good to his mother—and he's interested in young girls—and he hates to eat dinner alone. So there was nothing wrong with that, now was there ?

POP (*doubtfully*). I don't know now, Patricia——

PATRICIA (*hastily*). You know it's really an education to be with

Mr. O'Flaherty, Pop. Why, he told me something about chickens I never would have known if I hadn't gone to dinner with him!

MRS. HARRINGTON (*significantly*). H'm! Chickens!

PATRICIA (*eagerly*). Yes, Ma! A chicken is the only animal which is useful before it's born and after it's dead.

(POP *gives a cough.* PATRICIA *exchanges looks.*)

GRACE (*icily*). I'm waiting to hear why you cheated to win the cup!

PATRICIA (*to* POP). Well, we got talking about music at dinner and Mr. O'Flaherty told me Mr. Eisenwein was a great admirer of Victor Herbert.

POP. Yeah?

PATRICIA. Then we got talking about statesmen and politics and I found out Mr. Eisenwein thought Abraham Lincoln was the greatest statesman.

POP (*very interested*). Yeah?

PATRICIA. It was kind of hard to find out about the greatest financier. But the last time I was at dinner with him he told me Mr. Eisenwein was thinking of building a monument to Solomon.

POP. Which one?

PATRICIA. Chaim Solomon. Why, he was a Jewish gentleman. And if he hadn't loaned the Americans enough money to do it we never would have won the Revolutionary War.

POP. Oh! Yeah?

PATRICIA. So there you are! I said Chaim Solomon and Victor Herbert and Abraham Lincoln—and I won the cup!

MRS. HARRINGTON (*dramatically to* POP). There you are! There's the daughter you've raised!

GRACE (*furiously*). I never heard of such a thing! I never heard of such a thing in my life!

PATRICIA (*coldly—loftily*). I cannot permit your ignorance, however vast, to impeach my cleverness, however small! (*Coughs.*)

POP. What do you mean by that?

PATRICIA. I don't know myself. I just said it so she wouldn't know what I was talking about.

MRS. HARRINGTON (*rising and crossing*). As long as you got the cup dishonestly—why did you give it back? That's what I want to know! Haven't you got any sense at all?

PATRICIA (*appealing to* POP). I was so interested finding out if it would work I never thought how dishonest it was until I found I had won the cup!

POP. The next time you steal something—see me first before you confess.

PATRICIA. That isn't what you've always taught me, Pop. I leave it to you—it was the sportsmanlike thing to do, wasn't it?

POP. As a matter of fact—yes. (*Crosses down* L.)

MRS. HARRINGTON. There! You are sticking up for her.

You're to blame!　(*Crosses down* R.)　That's the way you've brought her up!

PATRICIA.　I don't think they were very good sports to put it in all the papers.

GRACE.　What are the nice people of the town going to think of us?

(POP *walks up and down.*)

(*To* POP.)　I told you not to let her join the Country Club!　I told you she'd do something that would make us all look like a lot of nobodies.　I told you, didn't I?　(*Glaring at* PATRICIA.)　I'll admit it's the only chance she had of getting a husband—out on the golf links!　(*She is very pleased with this dig.*)

PATRICIA (*with a smile,* L.C.).　Well—that's where most of them are!　(*Looks at her a moment with level eyes, then moving up* C.)

MRS. HARRINGTON (*sitting on settee.　*POP *walks up and down imitating her*).　Something like this always has to come up.　(*On the point of tears again.*)　If it isn't one thing it's another!

GRACE (*sarcastically*).　It's going to be a great pleasure going to the Country Club after this, isn't it?　What will the Caldwells think?

POP.　To hell with the Caldwells!

(*Telephone bell rings.*)

MRS. HARRINGTON.　Oh, William!

POP (PATRICIA *runs for 'phone*).　I'll answer it!　(*Crossing and taking off receiver.　Answers.*)　Hello?　Yes.　Who?　Miss Patricia?　Yes—she's here.

(*The positions are :　*POP *at 'phone above table* R.　MRS. HARRINGTON *on* L. *of settee.　*GRACE *down* R.　PATRICIA *up* C.)

(*Gruffly.*)　Hello?　Who is this speaking?　Mr. O'Flaherty?　What do you want with her?—Over to your house?　When do you mean—right now?　Yes, I saw the papers to-night—what about it?　What do you want to talk to her about?　Just a minute.　Here.　I can't get head or tail of it—he wants to talk to you.　(*Handing the 'phone to* PATRICIA.)

PATRICIA (*standing above table ;　*POP *moving to* L.C.　*At the 'phone with a look of despair*).　Hello?　(*Her voice is weak with fright.*)　Yes?　Do you have to see me to-night, Mr. O'Flaherty?　Wouldn't to-morrow do?　Well, I'll have to ask my father if I can go.　Just a minute, please.　(*Leaning 'phone on shoulder to cover it.*)　What'll I tell him, Pop?

POP.　Tell him you'll go.

PATRICIA (*frantically*).　I'm afraid to go.　I don't dare to face him.　I'd die!

POP (*sternly*).　Tell him you'll go!

PATRICIA (*wilts*).　Why don't you tell me I can't?

POP (*sternly*).　Go on—tell him!

PATRICIA (*into 'phone*). All right, Mr. O'Flaherty—I'll be right over! Yes, sir. (*Very slowly she hangs up.*)

POP (*crossing up for hat*). Come on—I'll go with you. It's right around here on Malcomb Avenue, isn't it?

PATRICIA (*weakly, quite crushed*). Yes, sir.

MRS. HARRINGTON (*rising, crosses*). Well! That's better! See that you do go with her. I won't have my daughter go to any man's house that talks about chickens!

(POP *crosses to door after getting his hat.* GRACE *delighted, crossing up above table to* C.)

PATRICIA (*she pauses with a new thought—turns and watches her father putting on his hat*). Say, Pop—I've put Mr. O'Flaherty in a terrible position—and anything he says to me I deserve. But you don't deserve to go over there and be humiliated on account of something I did. You don't have to go, Pop. I'll go alone.

POP. Never mind now. Anything he's going to say to you he's going to say it in front of me. I'll go with you. (*Moving to door* R.)

MRS. HARRINGTON. You can be sure he'll go. I wouldn't trust you alone! You probably wouldn't go! (*Rising and moving to* R.C.)

PATRICIA (*comes up to her—wistfully*). Aw, Ma—you know I would. And I'm—I'm awfully sorry it happened, Ma. I thought I was just doing something you'd be proud of.

GRACE. For God's sake! Don't ever do anything you think we might be ashamed of!

PATRICIA (*giving her sister a pained look—then wistfully turning to her mother*). Won't you believe me, Ma? I'm awfully sorry I did it. (*She rather timidly tries to put her hands on her mother's shoulder.*)

MRS. HARRINGTON (*turning and slapping her hands away from her*). Don't touch me! You've disgraced us!

(PATRICIA *wilts at this rebuke and backs away a little, staring at her mother, then to* GRACE.)

PATRICIA (*goes to door—turns—her old spirits assert themselves. She smiles*). We who are about to die, salute you! (*She makes a mock gesture of salute—*POP *does the same business—and turns.*)

(*Exit* POP *and* PATRICIA *door* R. *arm in arm.* MRS. HARRINGTON *sits on chair* L.C.)

GRACE (*glares after them—then turns to her mother*). What do you suppose Mr. O'Flaherty is going to do? Do you suppose he's going to make trouble?

MRS. HARRINGTON (*on verge of tears again*). I suppose so!

GRACE. Aren't you going over to Mrs. Hampton's to-night?

MRS. HARRINGTON (*whining*). No. I couldn't go anywhere to-night! I couldn't face people and have them talking about it.

I'm ill. I'm going to bed. If anyone calls just say that I'm indisposed.

GRACE. I'm not going to be here. I'm going out with Billy—if he ever gets here. He's half an hour late now. He's always late—and I'm getting sick of it.

MRS. HARRINGTON (*rises*). Well, it's your own fault if he's late.

GRACE (*snappishly*). How can I help it if he's late? (*Crossing down and sitting* L.C.)

MRS. HARRINGTON. Now's the time to begin, Grace. If he doesn't respect you enough to keep his appointments promptly now —he certainly never will after you're married. You've got to begin now! If you let him know he's got to be on time he'll be on time. You're very foolish if you let him do it.

GRACE (*peevishly*). Oh, don't lecture!

MRS. HARRINGTON. Oh, of course! Don't let your mother give you any advice. But if you don't take my advice—don't come to me afterward with your troubles. I'm warning you.

GRACE (*rising and crossing to above settee*). Oh, it's getting so I can't say a word in this house without having to listen to a lot of advice. I'll be glad when I'm out of it.

MRS. HARRINGTON. That's a nice thing to say to your mother! Now, isn't it?

GRACE (*sitting on settee*). Well, if you don't like it don't nag me and you won't hear me say things like that.

MRS. HARRINGTON (*astounded*). Nag at you! Oh, very well, Grace. I have nothing more to say. (*She turns and goes upstairs a few steps.*)

GRACE (*explosively*). Thank God!

MRS. HARRINGTON (*hysterically bursting into tears*). Oh, what have I ever done! What have I ever done to deserve this? (*As she goes upstairs.*) I wish I'd never been born!

(*Exits upstairs.*)

(GRACE *furiously looking after her—then glancing at wrist-watch. Going to the door and looking out. Then coming back slamming door viciously—working herself up into a fury. Then, as if struck with a sudden idea, she goes up to 'phone behind table and jerks receiver off the hook.*)

GRACE (*instantly starts jamming hook up and down*). Hello! (*She waits—growing more furious.*) Hello! (*She jams hook up and down again.*) What? The line is busy! I didn't give you the number yet! I did not. I said I did not. I didn't give you the number. Don't you tell me I did. I didn't. Is that so? Well, you're another. How dare you talk to me like that? What's your number? I don't care to hear anything more from you—I'm asking you for your number. Number four? Give me the chief operator. I won't give you the number. I want the chief operator.

(*She waits.*) Chief operator ? (*Her voice is now velvety and sweet.*) This is Miss Grace Harrington speaking. I was about to call a number from operator No. 4 a moment ago—in fact I waited over twenty minutes before the operator deigned to answer me. And when she did answer she informed me the line was busy—before I gave her the number. Yes, before ! I told her I hadn't given her the number yet and she called me a liar. Yes. I remonstrated with her very politely and she used the vilest language I ever heard over the telephone. Yes. Yes. No, I was very polite and patient with her. I dislike reporting her but I feel you ought to know because this is the fourth time recently that we've had trouble with her. I know it's the same girl because I always ask for her number. Yes. Thank you—I hope you will. (*She smiles a pleased, vengeful smile.*) Hello—I want three-seven-nine Lakewood, please. Thank you so much.

(*The sound of a motor is heard off* R.)

(*Pauses.*) You can keep your old number. I don't want it. (*She hangs up receiver, crosses to door, looks out. Closes door, moves to* L.C., *stiffens and angrily faces toward sound. A moment later door-bell rings.* GRACE *goes to door and opens it. Enter* BILLY CALDWELL *door* R.)

BILLY (*closing door*). Hello, dear—— (*Kissing her.* GRACE *moving away to* R.C.) What's the matter—am I late ?

GRACE (*without turning*). Aren't you even aware of it ?

BILLY. I'm sorry, dear, but something happened, and—— Where's Pat ? (*Crossing to stairs.*)

GRACE. It happens that she is not here.

BILLY. Say, I was just reading in the papers. (*Laughs, coming down to* GRACE *in front of sofa.*) Wasn't that the cutest trick she played on the intellectuals out at the Country Club ? I'm just tickled to death over it. Where is she ? I want to give her a kiss.

GRACE. What's that got to do with your being late ?

BILLY (*looks at wrist-watch*). I'm sorry, dear. But I'm—well—I got in a jam—and I've got to ask you to help me out.

GRACE (*coldly*). A jam ? What jam ? Are you always in a jam ?

BILLY. Well, now I'll tell you. You remember Sadie Buchanan, don't you ?

GRACE (*stiffens*). Naturally ! How could I forget her ? What about her ?

BILLY. She's in town again—visiting my cousin. Came unexpectedly—and Mary asked me to help her out to-night—she's in a jam herself—so I asked Sadie to come along with us. She's out in the car.

GRACE (*angrily*). Are you serious ?

BILLY (*fumbles a little*). Why—er—you know—I had to take her off Mary's hands—just for the evening. You don't mind—surely.

GRACE (*icily*). I'm surprised that you would dare to suggest such a thing, Billy. I didn't think you'd dare.

BILLY. Why ? What's the matter with Sadie ?

GRACE. Are you really asking me to go out on the same party with Sadie Buchanan—after the way she chased around after you and the way she snubbed me—and the things she said ? (*Crossing to L. and back to chair L.C.*)

BILLY. Oh, listen, Grace. I practically had to do it. My cousin begged me to do it. I'm just helping her out—that's all.

GRACE. I'm not as stupid as your cousin thinks I am, Billy. She doesn't like me—but you don't believe it. She knew what she was doing when she arranged this. (*Moving angrily up to stairs, then turning and coming down C.*) And if you think I'm going to humiliate myself before everyone by doing it, you're mistaken. I'm just as smart as your cousin is.

BILLY. You don't mean you won't go ?

GRACE. I certainly will not.

BILLY. Aw, Grace, come on—be a good fellow, will you ? I'm in a hell of a hole.

GRACE. Oh ! Now I'm not a good fellow !

BILLY. I didn't say that. But I'm in a fix—come on and help me, will you ?

GRACE. I wouldn't take a thousand dollars and be seen at the same party with her—after the things she said about me when you became friendly with me. You knew I wouldn't. (*Sitting L.C. chair.*)

BILLY. But I've told her you were going ! What's she going to think ?

GRACE. I'm not worrying about what she thinks. I'm worrying about what other people would think if I went. I don't care what she thinks. (*Turning away to L.*)

BILLY (*amazed—stops pleading and looks at her for a moment with a set face*). I invited her to go with us to-night—and I'm going to take her.

GRACE (*sneeringly over her shoulder*). I've told you to take her, haven't I ? I won't go with her—and you can go out and tell her so.

BILLY. All right ! You don't have to go. But I'll tell her nothing of the sort. I'll tell her you're sick and couldn't come—and that you asked to be excused—and sent your regrets.

GRACE (*rising in a fury*). Is that so ? All right, Mr. Caldwell, as long as you take that stand, if you go out with her to-night you can keep on going with her.

BILLY. You're talking like a crazy person !

GRACE (*turning away*). Oh, now I'm crazy, am I ?

BILLY. Don't twist everything I say into an insult !

(*There is a knock at the door* R.)

GRACE. Who's that, I wonder?

BILLY. I'll answer it. (*Crossing to the door and opening it.*) Oh, come in, Sadie.

(*Enter* SADIE BUCHANAN *door* R. SADIE *is a girl a little older than* GRACE, *well dressed, rather stylish and very agreeable.*)

SADIE (*pleasantly, coming forward to* GRACE). Oh, how are you, dear? I'm so glad to see you again.

GRACE (*coldly—and inwardly furious*). How do you do?

SADIE. I hope I'm not too bold. Billy tried to make me wait in the car; but I'm one of those nuisances who won't stay put. (*Sitting on settee, laughingly.*) I'm just dying for a cigarette, and there are three sweet old ladies on the front porch next door. I didn't want to scandalize the neighbourhood—do you mind—while we're waiting?

BILLY. Of course not. (*Eager to patch things.*) Here you are, Sadie. (*Handing* SADIE *cigarette and lighting it.*) Where'd you like to go to-night, Grace? Sadie and I have decided we'd leave it to you—er—didn't we, Sadie?

SADIE. It was so sweet of you, dear, to ask me to come.

GRACE (*coldly*). Did I?

SADIE (*taken aback*). Oh! Why—— (*Turning and looking at* BILLY—*then at* GRACE.) Didn't you?

GRACE (*over-sweetly*). Not that I remember!

BILLY (*shocked*). Grace!

GRACE. Billy must have quite misunderstood. I'm not going.

SADIE. Oh, I'm so sorry. Oh, please—I didn't understand. I wouldn't have this happen for anything. (*Rising and placing cigarette on ash-tray above settee.*)

BILLY. Grace! For Heaven's sake! What's the matter with you?

GRACE. You know very well what's the matter!

SADIE. Please, Miss Harrington—don't blame Billy. He fibbed to me about your asking me—but I forgive him. It was just a generous thought of his. And I won't allow your evening to be spoiled. (*Turning towards the door* R.)

BILLY. You're not going to spoil it. I'm sorry I said that—but I thought it would be all right, Sadie.

SADIE. Don't apologize, old dear. It's perfectly all right. I'm going to trot home. It isn't far and the walk will do me good.

BILLY (*furiously*). No, you're not. I won't let you walk home.

SADIE (*with a smile*). Don't you think it would be very, very good for my reputation to walk home from an automobile ride?—just once?

BILLY. You're not going to do it, I tell you. I'll take you—and I won't take you home, either.

GRACE (*furious*). Oh, won't you ?

BILLY. I certainly will not. If you refuse to come, Grace, that's your affair.

GRACE. It's also my affair to choose my associates.

SADIE. Oh, I'm sorry, Miss Harrington. (*Taking a step to* GRACE.) I didn't know you felt toward me like that. If I had known I shouldn't have embarrassed you by——

GRACE (*sneeringly*). I don't know that I'm particularly embarrassed !

(SADIE *at door* R., *ready to leave.*)

BILLY. Well, by God, I am !

GRACE (*sarcastically*). You'd better go, hadn't you ? Your old family friend is growing impatient.

BILLY (*with cold, set anger*). All right, I will go.

GRACE. Well, if you do, don't come back !

BILLY. All right, I'll go. Let me tell you something. I won't be back—either ! (*He stands a moment staring at her, then swiftly turns, opens the door and goes.*)

(*Exit* BILLY *and* SADIE *door* L.)

(GRACE *stands immovable for several moments as though expecting the sound of the auto starting and disappearing. Then she utters a cry of rage.*)

(MRS. HARRINGTON *enters at top of the staircase.*)

MRS. HARRINGTON (*coming down a few steps, speaking over banisters*). Heavenly days ! Were you and Billy quarrelling ?

GRACE (*putting on her wrap*). No. (*Angrily.*) We were fighting !

MRS. HARRINGTON. Oh, my heavens ! What about ?

GRACE. About plenty.

MRS. HARRINGTON. Haven't you any more sense than that ? What were you thinking about ? How could you do such a thing —what did you do ?

GRACE (*wheeling on her way to the door*). This is what I got for listening to your advice. You're the one that did it—not me ! (*She almost screams at her.*) You did it—you hear that ? You did it ! (*Sitting on settee, then jumping up and rushing to the door* R.)

MRS. HARRINGTON. Grace ! Where are you going ?

GRACE (*opening the door*). I'll show Billy Caldwell ! I'll show him !

MRS. HARRINGTON (*frantically*). Grace ! You come back here ! Grace !

(*Exit* GRACE *by door* R., *slamming the door after her viciously.*)

(*Comes down and sinks upon the sofa.*) Oh, my heavens ! (*She starts to weep. Sits.*) She's broken off her engagement to Billy

Caldwell. I don't know what I've ever done! What did I ever do to deserve this! Oh, my heavens!

(*Enter* Patricia *door* R. *She peeps in, sees her mother seated on the* L. *of settee, crying, seems undecided, then motions to someone behind her and enters.* Francis Patrick O'Flaherty *follows her in, shutting the door.* O'Flaherty *is a middle-aged man, very stout, and of genial countenance. He is dressed in a plain business suit and carries behind him a silver loving cup.*)

Patricia (*tenderly*). Ma, are you still feeling bad about it? I've got a gorgeous surprise for you.

Mrs. Harrington (*without lifting her head—wails*). What did Mr. O'Flaherty want you for?

Patricia. Mr. O'Flaherty's here, Ma. Here he is—right here.

Mrs. Harrington (*shocked—starting up*). What?

Patricia. My mother, Mr. O'Flaherty—this is Mr. O'Flaherty, Mother.

Mrs. Harrington (*does not rise—coldly*). How do you do, sir?

Patricia. I coaxed Mr. O'Flaherty to come over with me, Ma— to explain it.

O'Flaherty (*with a genial laugh*). Yes, Mrs. Harrington. You see, it's just a bit of a jest. That's why I didn't want to talk about it over the 'phone. (*Again laughing.*) Pat and I were just playing a little joke on the High Hats out at the Country Club.

Mrs. Harrington (*glaring*). Pat!

O'Flaherty (*not understanding*). I beg your pardon.

Mrs. Harrington (*glaring*). You should. So you're the one responsible for this disgrace, are you?

Patricia. Oh, Ma! No! Show it to her, Mr. O'Flaherty. See, I've won the cup. My name's engraved on it and everything. Mr. O'Flaherty knew about the cup all the time and Mr. Eisenwein said I had to keep it because I was honest enough to tell the truth and try to give it back. Show it to Ma, Mr. O'Flaherty.

Mrs. Harrington (*waving it away as she faces to* L.). I don't want to see it! It's just an insult to give you the cup now. Just an insult!

Patricia. No, it isn't, Ma. But Mr. O'Flaherty says I must never do it again for fear I'd get a very bad name—like the girl who married Mr. Jorgahod Bungleblotz.

(Mr. O'Flaherty *laughs heartily.*)

Mrs. Harrington. It's very funny, isn't it? I wish this idiotic joke was as funny to us as it is to Mr. O'Flaherty.

O'Flaherty. I beg your pardon.

Mrs. Harrington. As I said before—you should!

O'Flaherty. Now understand me, Mrs. Harrington. I'm not exactly begging anybody's pardon. I'm trying to find out what you said.

MRS. HARRINGTON.   The next time you think of a joke to play on somebody—play it on some other family.

PATRICIA.   Oh, Ma !

O'FLAHERTY (*still laughing and putting the cup on table behind settee and crossing down to* PATRICIA R.).   I think I'll be going, Pat. Something tells me your mother doesn't care about our little joke. But keep the cup just the same.

PATRICIA.   Thanks, Mr. O'Flaherty !

O'FLAHERTY (*winks*).   Good night. Good night, Mrs. Harrington.

MRS. HARRINGTON (*with great emphasis*).   Good night.

(*Exit* O'FLAHERTY *by the door* R.)

PATRICIA.   Oh, Ma—please don't feel so bad about it. It just kills me when I do something that makes you miserable. I feel like a regular crime wave.

MRS. HARRINGTON.   Every woman in the Country Club is going to hate us—that's what you've done !

PATRICIA   Just to show you how sorry I am—I'll do the dishes every day for six months—if you'll only say you forgive me.

MRS. HARRINGTON (*crying*).   You just seem to be possessed !

PATRICIA.   Well, I'm going to reform, Ma. Maybe you won't believe it—but I am.

MRS. HARRINGTON.   Huh !

PATRICIA.   I see where I made my mistake. When I was trying to think of something to give up for Lent—(*sitting on sofa*)—I gave up all my New Year's good resolutions.

MRS. HARRINGTON (*still wet-eyed*).   Where's your father ?

PATRICIA.   He had to go down town.

MRS. HARRINGTON (*cries*).   Down town. Oh, yes, down town spending money on himself !   Other people can have automobiles— and when I want to go anywhere I've got to ride in a street-car like a common washerwoman !   Between you and your father I don't know what's going to become of us. (*Relishing the misery.*) I wish I was dead !

PATRICIA (*impulsively—almost frightened—putting her arms around her*).   Ma ! Please don't wish you were dead ! If you were dead I'd never have another happy day in my life. Don't say things like that—it might come true ! Please take it back, Ma.

MRS. HARRINGTON (*impatiently throwing her hands from her*). Don't touch me ! Let me alone !

PATRICIA.   Ma, don't you believe I love you ? Don't you, Ma ?

MRS. HARRINGTON.   Then why do you do these damnable things ! You've never been anything but a curse to me since the day you were born.

PATRICIA (*standing, facing audience, cringing from the rebuke. She looks at her sniffling mother and bravely fights back the tears. She heaves a big sigh and then takes a calmer tone. Hastily*).   Well, there's no use crying over spilt milk, because there's enough water in it already.

MRS. HARRINGTON (*gasps. Rising*). Oh! If you don't stop saying things in this house, I'm going crazy! Do you hear? I'm going crazy! (*She starts for stairs.*)

PATRICIA. Oh, Ma!

MRS. HARRINGTON (*turning on the stairs*). What?

PATRICIA (*crossing up to L. of stairs*). Did Tony come here—or 'phone—while I was out?

MRS. HARRINGTON. Tony? You mean Tony Anderson?

PATRICIA: Yes. Did he? (*Crossing to window-seat R.*)

MRS. HARRINGTON. No, he didn't. What's he coming here for?

PATRICIA. He just said he might drop around to-night—if he wasn't doing anything.

MRS. HARRINGTON. What business has he coming here when he knows Grace is engaged to Billy Caldwell? Billy Caldwell won't like it. He hasn't any business coming here.

PATRICIA (*scared*). Why—he—he was coming to see me.

MRS. HARRINGTON. I don't want him coming here. And if you asked him to come this time—all right, but don't ask him again.

PATRICIA. Oh, but, Ma——

MRS. HARRINGTON. Don't answer me back. I won't have it. You've done enough DAMAGE NOW! THE NEXT THING YOU'LL break off Grace's engagement.

PATRICIA (*still on window-seat*). But can't he come to see me?

MRS. HARRINGTON (*angrily*). I said no—didn't I?

PATRICIA (*with a shrug*). Well, life is like that. All the world's a stage—but most of us are only stage-hands. (*Sits.*)

MRS. HARRINGTON (*almost shrieks*). There you go again! Oh! Oh!

(PATRICIA *jumps up. Exit* MRS. HARRINGTON *upstairs.*)

PATRICIA (*coming down*). Mom! Darn those darned books, anyhow!

(*The sound of a big car is heard off* R. PATRICIA *listens a moment and then running to the looking-glass* R. *and putting her hair straight, then going back and taking a final look. When bell rings* PATRICIA *crosses down, then just as she is about to open the door she stops and steps back to* R.C., *pulling her dress straight and then flinging door open.*)

Oh, hello, Tony. Oh, I'm so glad to see you. Come in.

(*Enter* TONY ANDERSON. *He is dressed in a very neat dark suit— different from suit worn in Act I. He looks, if possible, more handsome and attractive than ever, and* PATRICIA *devours him with her eyes as she closes the door.* TONY *is carrying a paper.*)

TONY (*cheerily*). Hello, Patricia. How are you? (*He throws hat on arm-chair up* L. *of stairs. Crossing to* c.) Won't be able to stay long—but I had to see you. Did you see the papers to-night ?

PATRICIA (*pulling up suddenly*). Gosh ! Didn't I, though ?

TONY. Were you surprised ?

PATRICIA. Wasn't I just ?—Were you ?

TONY (*staring*). No—I put it in.

PATRICIA (*sitting*). Huh ? You did ?

TONY. Yes. What are you talking about ?

PATRICIA. I'm talking about all the stuff that was in about me and that darned silver cup.

TONY (*with a laugh*). Oh, I saw that ! Good joke, wasn't it ? Handed me a big laugh. (*Crossing to settee and sitting on* L. *arm of same.*) That isn't what I meant. Didn't you notice anything else in the paper ?

PATRICIA. No. I was so busy with my own scandal I never even looked at anything else. (*Sitting on* R. *of sofa.*)

TONY. That accounts for it then. (*Up* L.C., *taking paper from pocket.*)

PATRICIA (*eagerly*). What, Tony ?

TONY. To-day is the day I put in the ads. for the opening of the new tract to-morrow. (*He unfolds newspaper.*) I spent a year laying out this tract—it's going to be one of the most beautiful in the country. How do you like the name of it ? (*Coming down to settee and handing her the paper.*)

PATRICIA (*looking and staring at him incredulously*). Tony !

TONY (*smiles*). Like it ?

PATRICIA (*dumbfounded*). Tony—you don't mean——

TONY (*moving to her and away again*). I never told a soul—I was going to name it after Grace. Of course now it might make Billy Caldwell sore. There it is, Patricia—there's your name on the prettiest development in the country.

PATRICIA (*stunned*). Patricia Park ! Tony—you're just wonderful !—that's all. I feel as if I wanted to cry. (*She almost does so. Kneeling on settee. One foot is seen to waggle.*)

TONY. You mustn't do that. (*Moving away and diving his hand into his inside pocket.*) Here. Here's something that goes with it. (*Handing her the deed.*)

PATRICIA. Tony ! What is it ?

TONY (*sitting by her side on her* L. *and smiling*). That's a deed to one of the best lots on the Circle of Patricia Park. What's the use of having a park named after you if you don't even own one lot in it ?

PATRICIA. Oh, I couldn't. I couldn't take this, Tony. It's just perfectly beautiful of you to think of it—but I couldn't.

TONY (*standing by the settee*). Too late now—it's recorded. See ? (*He points out record stamp.*) It's yours . . . a hundred by a hundred and fifty feet. It'll be worth money in a couple of years.

PATRICIA. Oh, but, Tony——

Tony. Please don't say anything, Patricia. It's just a little present from me to my best and sincerest girl friend—that's all. (*Moving away to up* L.)

Patricia. I wish I could say something, Tony.

Tony (*smiles*). I told you I was going to help you get that fellow you're in love with, didn't I?

Patricia. Uh-huh.

Tony (*coming down with a smile, then crossing away to* c. *to* L.). Well, this is part of it. Maybe he'll begin to sit up and take notice when he finds out a beautiful forty-acre tract is named after you.

Patricia (*beginning to see complications ahead*). Oh, gosh!

Tony. Well—what progress have you made? Have you seen him since?

Patricia (*thinking hard*). Well—just once—since you were here.

Tony. Does he seem to be more interested?

Patricia. Yes. Er—he's called on me.

Tony. Great.

Patricia. And he—he—gave me a beautiful present, too.

Tony. What'd I tell you? That's a darned good sign. It begins to look lucky. Did you try any of those things I told you on him?

Patricia. Well—er—I'm trying them.

Tony. Did you find out what he's interested in?

Patricia. Uh-huh.

Tony. Are you giving him lots of applause?

Patricia. I'm—er—I'm going to.

Tony. That's the stuff. Don't forget that—it's most important.

Patricia. I won't.

Tony (*sitting by her on settee*). And—did you remember what I told you about finding what his little pet dream is—and pulling for it?

Patricia. Uh-huh. Oh, dear, Tony! I think that little dream of yours is adorable.

Tony (*pleased*). About pouring the coffee in the morning?

Patricia (*gives him quick, searching look, then goes on*). Only a poet could have a dream like that. Every time I close my eyes I can see that exquisite little breakfast room—with painted furniture and white linen—and the girl sitting across the table from you—pouring your coffee. I adore it!

Tony (*pleased*). It is a sweet little idea, isn't it?

Patricia. It's so beautiful it's just a heart-breaker!

Tony (*dreamily*). Isn't it, though?

Patricia. You know something I always think of to go with it?

Tony (*eagerly*). What?

Patricia. On a cold, stormy night, with the wind howling outside and rattling the shutters—you and the girl—sitting before the fireplace—holding hands—and dreaming.

Tony (*looks at her a moment—looks straight out a moment—smiles*). You're a pretty good little dreamer yourself, aren't you ? (*Looking at her.*) O'Flaherty is a lucky man.

Patricia. O'Flaherty !

Tony (*smiles*). I've been figuring it out—and he's the only one it could be. He's the man you're in love with, isn't he ?

Patricia (*worried*). What makes you think that ?

Tony (*smiling*). Never mind—I know.

Patricia (*rising, crossing up and getting books from table above settee. Eager to change the subject*). Oh, before I forget, Tony—I got two books from the library on psychology—and I'm studying them.

Tony (*brightening*). Oh—have you become interested in psychology ? (*Rising and moving up c. to* Patricia.)

Patricia. I couldn't help it—after you told me how wonderful it is. But I guess it takes a brain as wonderful as yours to really understand it, Tony.

Tony (*obviously pleased and flattered*). Oh, yes—but I've been studying it a long time.

Patricia. Yes—but that's the point ! How many men would study it ? No wonder you're brilliant, Tony.

Tony (*very pleased*). Oh, I don't know. But it seems good to find somebody who doesn't think it's a bore.

Patricia (*gives him a swift glance. Puts books on table*). I adore it ! Tony, I just can't get over this ! (*Placing the deed on the table with the books.*) Nobody would think of doing a thing like this, only you !

Tony (*flattered*). Oh, well—I love to do little things for my friends.

Patricia. That's what I mean. You never think of yourself ! You're the most perfectly unselfish person I know !

Tony (*braces up, very pleased with himself*). Oh, I don't know—it's nice of you to say that, anyway.

Patricia. I suppose lots of people think you're opening up Patricia Park—gee ! I love to say that—Patricia Park !

Tony. Isn't it pretty ?—What were you going to say ?

Patricia. What ? I suppose lots of people think you're opening it up to make a lot more money—but I know the real reason.

Tony (*surprised*). What ?

Patricia (*they meet c.*). You weren't thinking of yourself. You were thinking of a lot of beautiful little bungalows and charming homes full of happy people—and—(*she smiles at him*)—and bright, cheerful breakfast rooms—and pretty girls sitting across the table in the mornings pouring coffee for their husbands. Weren't you ?

Tony (*obviously pleased*). Well—I—I——

Patricia. Yes, you were. Don't deny it. You couldn't help thinking something beautiful like that because you're just full of beautiful dreams, Tony—just like a poet.

TONY (*with an effort to be modest*). Well—I'm not going to lie to you, Patricia—but that really was my idea.

PATRICIA. I knew it. I told you you were wonderful, Tony—but you wouldn't believe it.

TONY. I'm not so *very* wonderful.

PATRICIA. You just say that because you're so modest. Anybody else would be going around bragging about it.

TONY (*flattered*). Oh! (*Taking a step away to L.*)

PATRICIA. You're the sort of man a woman could just simply adore, Tony.

TONY. None of them do, though.

PATRICIA. That's because none of them have found out what a beautiful soul you've got.

TONY (*moving closer*). Oh—I don't know—I never could talk to anybody else before like I'm talking to you. This is doing me a world of good—having you to talk to——

PATRICIA. It's doing me a lot of good, too.

TONY (*moving closer*). That little lonesome club of ours was a great idea, wasn't it?

PATRICIA. Wasn't it though?

TONY. You know, I've been thinking about it a lot. It seems to me as if you were some new person I'd never seen before—somehow.

PATRICIA. You're like that to me, too.

TONY. (*They are now quite close to each other.*) I hope it won't sound uncomplimentary—but I never realized how pretty you are, Patricia.

PATRICIA. Do you think so, Tony?

TONY. I certainly do. You've got the prettiest teeth and eyes —and when you smile—you're just devilishly pretty—that's all.

PATRICIA (*delighted—conveys she has just realized his lessons are working. By chair L.C.*). Thanks, same to you. Say, you promised to tell me some more things to do—you know.

TONY (*not a bit enthusiastically*). You mean—how to make this fellow you're in love with like you?

PATRICIA (*eagerly*). Uh-huh. Now, what do you do after you've given him a lot of applause?

TONY (*gloomily and seriously. Crossing R. and sitting on edge of couch*). Well, now I'll tell you, Patricia—I'm just beginning to realize the big responsibility of this thing. You're going to get him and he might turn out to be the wrong man.

PATRICIA (*anxiously*). Oh, no, he isn't the wrong one, Tony. I'm sure of that. He's the right one—I'm positive.

TONY (*gloomily*). Yes, and I'm helping him to get one of the sweetest and cutest girls in the whole town. I'll bet he wouldn't do that for me.

PATRICIA. I'll bet he would, Tony. That's just the kind of a fellow he is. That's why I love him.

TONY (*rising, hands in pockets, pacing about gloomily*). It's the darnedest funniest thing! Every time I find some girl I could like she's always in love with somebody else—or married to somebody —or going to marry somebody else.

PATRICIA (*who has been watching him delightedly—almost on the point of jumping up and confessing—restrains herself*). It is funny, isn't it, Tony?

TONY (*very miserably*). Nobody would suspect it, Patricia; but you have a lot of very deep understanding and sympathy.

PATRICIA. Have I, Tony?

TONY. Yes—and it'll probably be wasted on that big, fat porpoise! (*Sits.*) He won't appreciate it. (*Wheels.*) Oh, I'm sorry —I didn't mean to say that. He's probably a nice fellow—after you know him.

PATRICIA. Oh, yes, he is, Tony.

TONY (*turns*). Say! Does your father know about this fellow?

PATRICIA. Yes.

TONY (*disgustedly*). Does he approve of him?

PATRICIA. Yes. (*A slight pause—they both look at each other.*) Tell me what to do next, Tony.

TONY (*rising and crossing to R. a step, then up to C.*). Well, I said I'd do it, and I will. After you get him interested—let him find out there's somebody else who wants you.

PATRICIA. Make him jealous, you mean?

TONY (*gloomily*). Not exactly that. Here's the idea: The minute a man finds out somebody else wants a girl he becomes a lot more anxious not to let anybody else have her. I know because I'm that way myself. (*Up C.*)

PATRICIA (*eagerly*). Uh-huh. (*Sitting on chair L.C.*)

TONY. So the next thing is to let him know somebody else is in love with you—and that you're almost in love—or pretty much in love with this somebody yourself.

PATRICIA. Oh, he thinks that already. I told him I'm crazy about somebody.

TONY. How'd he take it?

PATRICIA. He doesn't seem to think much of it.

TONY. You mean he doesn't care?

PATRICIA. No, I mean he doesn't like it.

TONY. I don't blame him.

PATRICIA. And then what next, Tony?

TONY (*coming behind chair L.C.*). Look here, Patricia—does your mother know about this?

PATRICIA. No. I haven't told her yet.

TONY (*firmly*). Then I've got to think this thing over before I go any further. It's working too darned well.

PATRICIA (*rising*). Aw, Tony, please.

TONY (*looking at his watch*). No! Besides, I've got to go. (*Moving up and getting his hat from arm-chair up L. and crossing to*

R., *then turning back.*) Say, are you going to the Country Club dance Friday night ?

PATRICIA (*worried*). I don't know. Are you ?

TONY. Yes. Don't tell anybody. I've decided to learn how to dance and I've taken a couple of lessons. Will you give me a dance—a couple of dances—that is, if you go ?

PATRICIA. Yes. Yes, I guess I will go, Tony.

TONY (*crossing to door, hand on the handle*). All right—I'll be looking for you Friday night. (*He suddenly comes to her.*) Who is it, Patricia ? (O., *appealingly.*) It is O'Flaherty, isn't it ?

PATRICIA (*shaking her head*). No, it isn't, Tony. It isn't Mr. O'Flaherty—honestly.

TONY (*has been twisting his hat round and round during this scene.*) Who is it, then ?

PATRICIA (*flustered*). I'll tell you some time—soon.

TONY. Will you ?

PATRICIA. Yes.

(*He studies her seriously a moment, then puts his hands on her shoulders and solemnly looks into her eyes, drawing her towards him. She realizes she is to be kissed and puts up her lips. He is just about to kiss her when he stops.*)

TONY (*turning his head away almost sadly, twisting his hat round*). No ! It wouldn't be right to kiss you. It isn't fair to you—or to him, either. Wouldn't be right.

PATRICIA. I don't think it would be wrong, Tony. (*Disappointedly, seeing she is going to miss the kiss.*) If you knew who it was— I'm sure it would be all right with him, Tony.

TONY (*smiling and facing her again*). Well, come to think of it there's nothing wrong in a couple of good friends—real friends— kissing each other.

PATRICIA. I should say not ! (*Makes careless what's-the-difference gesture.*) Shucks ! What's a kiss ? (*Turning away, but watching him out of the corner of her eye.*)

TONY (*suddenly throwing his hat on settee, he pulls her to him and kisses her. He is releasing her when he suddenly crushes her to him again and this time gives her a long, smothering kiss. Impulsively her arms go around his neck and she clings to him. They hold. Then, as if ashamed, he breaks away, picks up his hat and hurries to the door.*) Good night, Patricia. (*He goes without another word—hastily, leaving the door wide open.*)

PATRICIA. Good night, Tony.

(*Exit TONY door R. PATRICIA stands in a trance of happiness and awe.*)

(*The motor starts and dies away in the distance.*)

(*Standing in the doorway clapping her hands with joy, then closes the door.*) It works ! It works ! He loves me ! (*She stands round-*

eyed for several moments, again looking straight out, a picture of awe and wonderment. Suddenly a new thought seems to strike her. She smiles and says aloud, musingly.) Mrs. Tony Anderson! Mrs. Tony Anderson! (*The door flies open with a bang. Enter* GRACE *door* R. *She stops short inside the door and slams it shut, looking straight at* PATRICIA. *Her face is a picture of anger and fury. She frantically throws off her coat and hat and slams them into a chair—all the while facing the astonished* PATRICIA.) Grace! What's the matter? What's happened?

GRACE (*venomously*). You've broken off my engagement with Billy Caldwell—that's what's happened!

PATRICIA (L.C., *aghast*). Grace!

GRACE. Don't stand there like a ghost looking at me. You're the one who did it! You're the one who did it!

PATRICIA. Grace—you don't mean—why, he didn't do anything like that—he couldn't——

GRACE. He did—I tell you! (*Sitting on settee.*)

PATRICIA. I can't believe it—it's impossible. You didn't do anything. How can he blame you? Besides—everybody considers it as a joke—why, Mr. Eisenwein himself——

GRACE. A joke—yes. And they consider us a joke, too. That's what you've done.

PATRICIA. Well, I'll go to him and explain it. I'll go and see him——

GRACE (*angrily*). No, you won't. No, you won't see him. You'd love to go to him and humiliate me that much more, wouldn't you?

PATRICIA (*miserably*). Oh, Grace! I feel terrible. I'd almost give my life if it hadn't happened.

GRACE (*stiffening and staring at her*). What was Tony Anderson doing here?

PATRICIA (*starting and staring as she realizes the meaning of the question*). He came here to call on me, why?

GRACE (*rising*). Oh, he came to call on you, did he? Well, he isn't coming here to call on you any more. When he comes here again he's coming to call on me.

PATRICIA (*straightens up*). Oh, no, he isn't!

GRACE (*around table*). You heard what I said, didn't you? You broke off my engagement to Billy Caldwell, so now I'm going to marry Tony Anderson.

PATRICIA (*quietly*). No, you're not. I'm going to marry Tony myself.

GRACE. You! You have a wonderful opinion of yourself, haven't you? All I'd have to do is give him a pleasant look and he'd forget there ever was such a person as you!

PATRICIA. That used to be so, but it isn't any more. You're not clever enough to take him away from me. And besides, Tony Anderson doesn't love you any more.

GRACE. Oh, he doesn't, eh? I suppose you've been telling him all the nasty, hateful lies you could invent about me. Is that the reason ? And I wonder where Papa's sweet little Sunday-school girl, who never cared about the boys, suddenly got so wise about men. Huh ! The family beauty is going to marry Tony Anderson. I hope you're not overlooking the fact that your face would stop a clock.

PATRICIA. Your face wouldn't stop a clock. Your face would make a clock run.

GRACE. Is that so ! Well, you heard what I said, didn't you ? I'm going to marry Tony Anderson.

PATRICIA. Grace, everything I've ever had you've wanted. And everything you've wanted, you've taken away from me. But you're not going to take Tony. He's the only boy I've ever loved. He's the only thing I've ever really wanted—he's the only thing in my life that's worth fighting for—and I'm going to fight—you understand—I'm going to fight ! (*Crossing up to stairs.*) And even if I didn't love him at all, I'd marry him just to save him from you. (*Running up two or three steps.*)

GRACE. You go to hell——

PATRICIA (*turning on stairs*). You run your own errands.

(PATRICIA *runs off.*)

Time of representation : 45 minutes.

ACT III

SCENE.—*Same as Act I. It is evening, after dinner, the next Friday night.*

At rise.—POP *dressed in his street attire, paces back and forth across the room. He is indignant, bristling, muttering to himself. He pauses, picks up a newspaper, makes a speech to himself, silently, and slams the paper down again for emphasis.*

Enter MRS. HARRINGTON *from door* L. *She is dressed to go out—in evening dress—but, for purposes of a quick change, she wears over this dress a heavy dressing-gown. She is carrying a pair of curling-irons and slams the door after her, and then stops to glare at* POP.

MRS. HARRINGTON (*starts as though to go upstairs—then changes her mind and addresses herself to* POP). After this don't interfere. I said she couldn't go to the Country Club dance and I don't want to hear any more about it from anybody.

POP (*appealingly*). Oh, May!

MRS. HARRINGTON. I said I didn't want to hear any more about it.

(POP *gives her a hard look and nods his head up and down.*)

Are you aware what time it is?

POP (*coldly*). Absolutely.

MRS. HARRINGTON. You'd better hurry up and get shaved and dressed, do you hear?

POP. If Pat can't go to the dance I don't go, either!

MRS. HARRINGTON (*staring at him*). What?

POP. You and Grace can go alone or get somebody else to take you. I won't do it. (*Crossing down* R.)

MRS. HARRINGTON (L.C.). If you think you can bluff me into letting her go you're mistaken. She's not going. And you go upstairs and get dressed, do you hear?

POP (*turning to her*). Now look here, May——

MRS. HARRINGTON. Uh, uh, uh, don't argue with me. I said she can't go and that finishes it.

POP. Oh, no, it don't. If she isn't going that just begins it.

MRS. HARRINGTON. You heard what I said—she can't go.

POP (*defiantly, moving* C. *to* R.). If she wants to go, she can go—and there ain't nobody here's going to stop her.

MRS. HARRINGTON. Oh, you're going to encourage her to defy me, are you ?

POP. You're damned right, I am. This is a rotten deal and she doesn't have to stand for it. (*He goes to the door* L. *and calls off.*) Pat—Pat—if you want to go to that dance, put on your things and go—and I'll take you. (*Coming back to* R.C.)

MRS. HARRINGTON (*runs to door*). Pat—you heard what I told you ! (*Slamming door and back to* C.)

POP (*shouting*). Leave those dishes. I'll do them myself. Put on your things.

MRS. HARRINGTON (*screams*). Pat—don't you dare !

POP (*in cold, furious anger, puts his fists on his hips and glares at her*). It was all right for Pat to go to the dance until Grace found out that Tony Anderson was going to be there, wasn't it ?

MRS. HARRINGTON. Grace had nothing to do with this !

POP. Don't pull that stuff on me—I know who started all this. Grace told her you wouldn't let her go to the dance before you knew anything about it.

MRS. HARRINGTON. That's a story—she didn't !

POP (*loudly*). I heard her myself. Grace started this—and it's one thing she started that she don't get away with——

GRACE (*upstairs—so near it is evident she has been listening*). Mother ! MOTHER ! Don't argue with him ! Don't argue with him.

POP (*furious*). Is that so ? (*Crossing up to stairs.*) You come on down here if you think you're smart enough to win this argument ! I dare you to come down here ! I'll box your ears for you ! (*Rushing up to stairs.*)

MRS. HARRINGTON (*crossing to* R.C., *screaming*). Grace, don't come down. Don't come down. He's gone off his head ! Don't you come down here ! Open the side window and call Mr. Brinckley !

POP (*turning on her and shouting*). Go ahead and call him ! Call the whole damned neighbourhood if you want to !

MRS. HARRINGTON (*comes down* C. *Aghast*). William ! What's the matter with you ? Are you in your right senses ?

POP. The time has come for somebody round this house to act like a man and I'm going to do it if I have to wreck the joint.

(POP *takes three steps towards her, she backing and waving the irons at him.*)

MRS. HARRINGTON. Don't you strike me !

POP (*amazed—walks slowly and threateningly toward her*). Did I ever strike you ?

MRS. HARRINGTON (*now really scared*). Don't you dare to strike me !

POP (*roars*). Did I ever strike you ?

MRS. HARRINGTON (*shrinks—frightened—backs to* L.). No, no, you didn't !

POP. Then you'd better keep your mouth shut. You're putting bad ideas in my head !

MRS. HARRINGTON (*circling round him to* R. *Afraid*). What !

POP (*menacingly*). Are you going to keep still and listen to what I'm going to tell you ? Are you ?

MRS. HARRINGTON (*gasping weakly and backing away to* R.). Yes.

POP (*menacingly*). All right then—don't open your mouth till I get done. Do you understand that ?

MRS. HARRINGTON (*meekly and with sobs. Gasps*). Yes, William ! (*Sinking on to settee.*)

POP (*crosses to long table*). All right. Pat didn't ask to come into this house. It isn't her fault that she's here. We brought her into this house and it's her home. It belongs to her just as much as it does to you and Grace—as long as she wants to stay in it. From now on she is going to cease to be the Patsy in this family. And she's going to get a square deal—and I'm going to see that she gets it. Do you get me ?

MRS. HARRINGTON (*meekly*). Yes !

POP (*shouting at the top of his voice*). All right. And while I'm at it I'm going to tell you something else ! For twenty-five years you've been whining, and nagging, and bawling, and weeping and making everybody's life miserable—now I'm going to be the doctor. The first time I hear a yupe out of you I'm going to break up the inside of this house and throw it out in the front yard. (*Moving up* O.)

(PATRICIA *enters door* L. *She comes through the door with a plate and drying towel in her hand—as though just washing the dishes. She is dressed in a very pretty evening dress—but over it is a cover-all apron.*)

PATRICIA (*miserable*). Pop, please stop !

POP (*with a wave of his arm*). Stop nothing !

PATRICIA. Please, Pop ! I never said a word—so why should you fight about it ? I don't want to go to the dance.

POP. If you won't fight your own battles and stick up for yourself I'm going to do it for you !

PATRICIA (*pleading*). Pop, please !

POP (*starting and looking at her seriously. Pointing to door* L.). Go on out there and do them there dishes.

PATRICIA (*gives him a startled look and meekly goes*). Yes—Pop !

(*Exit* PATRICIA *door* L.)

MRS. HARRINGTON (*with the anguished air of a martyr*). I wish I were dead !

POP (*hunches himself as he again puts his hands on his hips and takes a step toward her*). What's that ?

MRS. HARRINGTON (*scared*). What ?

POP (*repeats menacingly*). What was that you said ?

MRS. HARRINGTON (*frightened*). Nothing, William—nothing!

POP (L.C. *savagely*). I know it wasn't—but don't say it again. (*Pointing to the stairs.*) Go on upstairs and take Grace to the Country Club.

(MRS. HARRINGTON *crosses sobbing to the stairs.*)

Or go to bed sick—or do anything you damn please. Go on!

MRS. HARRINGTON. (*Giving a violent jump and with a scared and bewildered air runs to the staircase, but after going up a few stairs she seems to come to herself again. She pauses and looks at him*). This is the finish, William! (*Sob.*) You have nobody to blame but yourself. (*Sob.*) You're the cause of it all. (*Sniff.*) The days of barbarism are past. Cousin Percy has always told me any time I wanted a divorce he'd handle the case for nothing. (*Sniff.*)

POP (*below table*). I've heard that so often I'm sick of hearing it. (*Shouting.*) Go on upstairs.

MRS. HARRINGTON (*jumping again and running up three or four stairs*). I'm in earnest, William. This is the end. I've suffered too much. To-morrow I'm going to Cousin Percy.

POP (*roars*). All right—go on to your Cousin Percy—go on and get your divorce. And you can't get it soon enough to suit me. Go ahead and get your divorce. I'll go to-night.

(*Enter* PATRICIA *door* L. *She comes empty-handed this time, but scared and miserable. She stops* C. *to* L.)

PATRICIA (*pleadingly*). Ma! Pop! Please—please stop fighting over me. Don't you realize how miserable I feel when you fight about me? Please, Pop.

MRS. HARRINGTON (*angrily*). Yes, and who was the cause of it? Who causes all the trouble in this house?

PATRICIA (*wilts at this*). Please, Ma. (*Suddenly her emotions overcome her. She goes to the* L. *end of sofa with her arm crooked over her face and sinking down on it silently cries.*)

MRS. HARRINGTON. You ought to cry!

POP (*roars*). Hush! (*He glares at* MRS. HARRINGTON *and then comes awkwardly to the* L. *of the sofa. Exit* MRS. HARRINGTON *upstairs.*) Don't cry, Baby! This had to come some time and the sooner it's over the better.

PATRICIA (*sobs and clings to him*). No! You mustn't go. I don't want you to go.

POP (*obviously for the benefit of the listeners upstairs—turns his head a little toward them and talks loudly*). No use, Patricia. Only time I'm happy is when I go away—only time I'm unhappy is when I have to come back. The minute I walk in the door the misery starts. (*Louder, crossing up* C.) And let me tell you one thing else, and I don't care who hears me, if it wasn't for you there's a lot of times I never would have come home.

PATRICIA (*sobs*). Oh, Pop, please.

POP. I'm going out and walk around. (*Up by* L. *of the staircase.*) I've got to cool off. I've got a temperature of five hundred and ninety. Only trouble is I got it twenty-five years too late. (*Getting hat from cupboard.*)

PATRICIA (*jumps up and gets her arms around his neck. She kisses him*). Pop, you mustn't go away. You mustn't leave Ma. I'll just die if you go away.

POP (*gives a furtive look around toward stairs, then with his finger on his lip he smiles an expansive smile*). Ssh!

PATRICIA (*quietly*). Huh?

POP (*gives another cautious look and then winks a long wink*). Ssh!

PATRICIA (*hugs him again*). Oh, Pop!

POP (*lifting her in his arms and kissing her*). Ssh! (*He opens the door, still smiling.*)

(*Exit* POP *door* L. *He slams the door after him violently.*)

(PATRICIA *sits on the couch and begins to remove the evidences of tears with her handkerchief. After a moment she stops—looks straight out a moment—and then does one of those sighs peculiar to young girls after a crying spell—three gasping intakes of breath and an audible exhalation. Enter* GRACE *down the stairs. She is in evening clothes, ready for the dance, and again wears* PATRICIA'S *wrap. She comes as though having heard the slam of the door—but pauses on the stairs to take a look to see that her father is not there. Then she comes down to* PATRICIA—*still on the sofa.*)

GRACE. Where's Father?

PATRICIA. He's gone.

GRACE (*pausing* L. *of sofa and glaring at* PATRICIA). Now see what you've done. (PATRICIA *smiles at her.*) You've done everything else you could—(*putting wrap on sofa*)—now you've separated your own father and mother!

PATRICIA (*looking at her coolly a moment*). Some day somebody is going to sprinkle insect powder on you!

GRACE. You don't say so! (*Going to 'phone.*) Hello, well, it's about time you answered. Give me Grant five double nine.

PATRICIA (*noticing wrap*). Are you going to wear that wrap of mine again?

GRACE. Yes, I am. I suppose you're going to start another row about it.

PATRICIA. Nope. Go right ahead and wear it. I don't want it. You can have it. It's yours. I make you a present of it.

GRACE. Thanks.

PATRICIA. You're welcome.

GRACE. Hello, taxi company! This is 436 Linden Avenue, Harrington is the name. Can you send a taxi immediately? Well, we want it right away. And we don't want to wait for it. How long? Well, tell the man to get here as quick as he can. (*Smiling a nasty smile. Puts wrap up* L.C.) So you're not going to the dance after all, are you?

PATRICIA. Nope.

GRACE. I told you you weren't, didn't I?

PATRICIA. Yes.

GRACE. Maybe the next time you'll believe me!

PATRICIA. No, I won't. There isn't going to be any next time.

GRACE. Oh, isn't there?

PATRICIA (*quietly*). Nope! I won't be here the next time. You can have it all to yourself and do anything you like. (*Rising.*) There won't be anybody to interfere.

GRACE (*sarcastically*). Oh, I suppose you're going to leave home now.

PATRICIA (*quietly*). Yes. That's just what I'm going to do. (*Walking up and down.*) I make too much trouble in this place —somehow—and I got Ma and Pop fighting over me—(*struggling to keep back her tears*)—and I've never been anything but a curse to Ma ever since I was born—(*with some resentment showing through coming tears*)—and she never wanted me anyway—— (*Putting the handkerchief to her eyes and turning her head away, silently cries.*)

GRACE (*vindictively*). You ought to cry! You ought to cry! And if I had the authority I'd give you something to cry for!

PATRICIA (*dropping her hands and looking at her. She stares a moment, vengefully, and then, steadily glaring at her, slowly rises. She reaches her height and then slowly starts to move toward* GRACE *as though she intended tackling her*). You would—would you? (*Crosses slowly.*)

GRACE (*who has maintained an attitude of fearless defiance, suddenly loses her nerve and runs up to staircase, calling loudly*). Mother! Mother! Mother!

PATRICIA (*getting to stairs first. Frightened—instantly in a panic of whispered pleading to prevent more trouble*). Grace! Please don't, will you? Please! I was only fooling! Please!

MRS. HARRINGTON (*at head of stairs*). What's the matter down there?

PATRICIA (*pleadingly—whispers—runs upstairs*). Grace! (*She makes a frantic sign.*)

MRS. HARRINGTON (*more insistently*). Answer me! What's the matter down there? Grace!

GRACE. Pat was going to strike me!

MRS. HARRINGTON (*furiously*). She what?

GRACE. She ran after me and was going to strike me!

H

PATRICIA. Ooo, Ma! I was not. I was not! (*Changes to defiance.*) I was going to knock her so cold a glass of ice-water would scald her!

MRS. HARRINGTON. Don't you dare touch your sister—don't you dare.

GRACE (*with a pleased little grimace*). H'm! Smarty!

PATRICIA (C., *very quietly*). All right, Grace, all right. I was going to do the sportsmanlike thing to-night. But now I won't. As soon as you go I'm going to do you a dirty trick!

GRACE (R.C.). What do you mean?

PATRICIA (*laughs in spite of herself. She pauses*). I mean something about Tony Anderson.

GRACE (*smiles*). What will you bet he doesn't come home with me to-night?

PATRICIA. I won't bet. (*Turning from her with a sneer.*) You wouldn't pay a bet if you lost.

GRACE. Just the same I'll bet he comes home with me.

PATRICIA. Suppose he does. But that won't make any difference. If he comes home with you a hundred times—I'll take him away from you just the same.

GRACE (*sneeringly*). After to-night he won't as much as give you a pleasant look, you insignificant little gnat.

PATRICIA. No? All right. This is a case of mind over matter, dearie. I don't mind what you say—because you don't matter.

(PATRICIA *exits door down* L.)

(*Enter* MRS. HARRINGTON *down the stairs. She is dressed now in evening clothes and a wrap—and is still dabbing at her eyes and powdering—crying.*)

MRS. HARRINGTON. Did you order the taxi?

GRACE (*irritably*). Yes——

MRS. HARRINGTON. Where's Patricia?

GRACE (*nods toward dining-room* R.). In there. Do you want her?

MRS. HARRINGTON (*sits on sofa. Repowdering*). No!

GRACE. She told me as soon as I go she's going to do me some dirty trick. I don't know what she means.

MRS. HARRINGTON. Why don't you leave her alone?

GRACE (*peeved*). Oh, for Heaven's sake! Don't you start now!

MRS. HARRINGTON. Yes, and don't you start! Or you can go to the dance alone! So there!

GRACE (*turns and looks at her mother in tired disgust. Crosses* R.). Oh, my God! It's getting so nobody can open their mouth in this house without starting a war!

MRS. HARRINGTON. Do you want to go to that dance alone or don't you?

GRACE. You know I can't very well go alone!

MRS. HARRINGTON. Well, you keep on and you won't go at all

then. I'm in no condition to go anywhere. I ought to be in bed this minute. I'm ill ! (*She starts to give way to tears again.*)

GRACE (*wildly*). Oh, for Heaven's sake ! You're going to look a sight !

MRS. HARRINGTON (*with breaking voice*). I'd like to know why I wouldn't look a sight—the things I've got to put up with. (*Moving up to look in glass.*)

GRACE (*crosses to her mother*). Well, go on upstairs and go to bed if you want to. I'll go alone. You can't go with your nose all swelled up and your eyes red ! Either stop crying or go to bed !

MRS. HARRINGTON. Yes, and who made my eyes red ?

GRACE. I didn't do it. Don't blame it on me !

MRS. HARRINGTON. Well, do you want me to go or not ?

(*Motor is heard in distance, then coming nearer and stopping at door.*)

(*Enter PATRICIA door L. She has taken off the apron and now appears in the pretty evening dress.*)

GRACE. Oh, piffle ! I don't care what you do !

(*PATRICIA backs away a little with stricken face, watching her wistfully.*)

(*The door-bell rings.*)

There's the taxi. Stop crying, will you ? You're a sight ! (*She opens the door.*)

MRS. HARRINGTON. He's going away and leave me. (*Sinking on to settee.*)

(*Enter " TRIP " BUSTY door R. He stands at first just in the doorway. He is rather a tough-looking person in the forties, wearing a chauffeur's cap.*)

TRIP. Taxi ?

GRACE. All right. We'll be out in a minute.

TRIP (*sticks his head well in, looking at MRS. HARRINGTON*). Where'bouts you folks want to go ?

GRACE. I don't see how it can make any possible difference to you where we want to go.

TRIP. Well, it might make some difference to you—if it's some place I don't want to take you.

GRACE (*to MRS. HARRINGTON*). Did you ever hear anything like that ? (*To TRIP.*) You're supposed to take us to any place we tell you to.

TRIP. Oh, no, I'm not, Missus. I'm asking you where you want to go.

GRACE. We want to go to the Country Club.

TRIP. Well, couldn't you said that in the first place ?

GRACE. Such impertinence ! I'm going to report you. What's your name ?

TRIP (*grins—defiantly*). My name's Trip Busty.

GRACE. Who's the man who owns this taxi company?

TRIP (*grins*). I am, lady. I happen to be the boss myself.

GRACE (*glaring*). Would you mind waiting in the taxi, please?

TRIP (*grins*). It's all right with me, lady. The meter's ticking.

(*Exit* TRIP BUSTY R.)

GRACE (*closing door*). Come on. You can do that on the way, can't you?

MRS. HARRINGTON. I loved him so—— (*Hastily dabbing eyes.*) I don't know whether I ought to go or not.

GRACE (*snaps*). We're going to have to pay for keeping the taxi waiting. Come on, will you?

MRS. HARRINGTON (*rising*). I'm coming, ain't I?

GRACE. Then for God's sake hurry up!

(*Exit* GRACE *and* MRS. HARRINGTON *door* R.)

(PATRICIA *stands still watching them. The taxi door slams. The sound of a taxi is heard starting and then dying away. She listens, motionless, until the taxi cannot be heard, then a little smile plays over her lips as she thoughtfully looks straight out. She turns up and goes to the telephone, and takes receiver off hook.*)

PATRICIA. Hello.—Give me Lake View eight-seven.—Hello, Ellwood Country Club? Is this you, George? Would you please connect me with the parking stand? That's a good boy. (*A pause.*) Hello, is this the parking stand? Who is this speaking? Mr. McGinnis.—Well, Mr. McGinnis, this is Pat Harrington. Do you remember me? (*Pause.*) I'm fine, thanks. How are you? Why, could you do me a wonderful favour, Mr. McGinnis? Well, when Tony Anderson's car gets there—I wonder if you would—— (*She starts.*) What! Oh! he is? (*Pause.*) Well, Mr. McGinnis, please let me speak to him over your 'phone, before he goes into the club house. Thank you so much. (*Gives a little dance.*) Hello, Tony, this is Patricia—uh-huh.—I wanted to tell you, Tony—that I can't be there to-night.—Oh, I got in bad and Ma made me stay home—all alone.—No, honestly, Tony—I have to stay home all night, all alone. I wanted to tell you how disappointed I am because I've got to see you about something awfully important.—Uh-huh! Uh-huh! Yes, it's about him. Something very serious has happened. I'm in trouble and I can't tell you over the telephone.— Huh! Oh, I wouldn't want you to miss the dance.—No, Tony, I —— Well, of course if you insist—all right, Tony.—Yes.—Good-bye. (*Hanging up receiver and instantly standing and looking straight out—then a smile steals across her face.—Crossing and sitting on settee.*)

(*Enter* POP *door* R. *He comes in a brighter mood. There is a lightness*

*in his step. He is a new man. His chest is sticking out a bit.
He is all smiles.*)

Pop. Have they gone ?
Patricia. Who——
Pop. The folks——
Patricia. Yeh.
Pop. Thank God.
Patricia. Pop, I've got to talk to you about something, Pop.
Pop (*hanging his hat in cupboard and speaking cheerily*). What ?
(*Coming* c. *to* Patricia.)
Patricia. I've decided that I'm going to get a job somewhere,
Pop—and go somewhere else to live. And I want you to help me
get the job.
Pop (*sticking his thumbs in his vest and smiling at her*). Nothing
doing. You're going to stay right here, Baby. But it's never going
to be like it has been. You'll never know it's the same place.
Patricia (*surprised*). Huh !
Pop. From now on this is going to be a home—a home for you
and a home for all of us ! You're going to love to live here.
Patricia (*round-eyed and suspicious*). Huh ?
Pop (*moving up* c. *and down* L., *then back to* c.). I've made a great
discovery—it took me twenty-five years to do it but I finally did it.
(*He turns in his pacing.*) You think your mother is to blame
because she's always crying and complaining. She's not to blame.
She's right. She has a right to cry—she has a right to complain.
She's not to blame.
Patricia (*amazed*). Pop, where have you been and what have
they been giving you ?
Pop (*turns away*). Your mother is a wronged woman !
Patricia (*open-mouthed*). What !
Pop. I've wronged your mother. I've deceived her !
Patricia (*rising and moving to him*). Gracious ! Pop ! You
mustn't tell anybody. You must keep it quiet.
Pop (c.). Wait till I explain this to you ! Your mother wasn't
like this before I married her ! She was a wonderful girl. She was
as fine a girl as ever lived. I'm to blame for the way she is !
Patricia (*bewildered*). Pop !
Pop. She thought she was marrying a man ! She thought she
was going to have a husband ! And what did she get ?
Patricia. I don't know—what ?
Pop. She got a big fat slob who did everything his mamma told
him—like a nice little Sunday-school boy !
Patricia (*stunned*). Huh ?
Pop. Instead of acting like a man I acted like a darned coward.
No wonder she's disappointed and discontented. I treated her so
nice she never realized she was married. (*With great emphasis.*)
But wait till you see what happens from now on !

PATRICIA. But, Pop——

POP (*roars and points to sofa*). Sit down!

PATRICIA (*round-eyed—suddenly sits*). Huh!

POP (*halts and laughs*). It's all right, Baby. I was just practising—wait till she gets home. She's going to just love me.

PATRICIA. But, Pop, maybe——

POP. Maybe nothing. Did you see what happened to-night? For the first time in twenty-five years I acted like a regular husband and she nearly dropped dead of surprise.

PATRICIA. I hope you're right, Pop.

POP. I know I'm right. And there's a lot of other things I'm going to straighten out around this house. (*Up and down.*) Say, didn't you have a date with Tony Anderson at the Country Club? Aren't you going to the dance?

PATRICIA. Oh, it's all right, Pop. He was talking to me a few minutes ago—and—er—when he found I wasn't going—why—he's coming here.

POP (*looks at her keenly and a smile creeps over his face*). When Grace and your mother get out there he won't be there, huh?

PATRICIA (*smiling a little guiltily*). Well—no!

POP (*delightedly*). How'd he come to telephone? I don't suppose you had anything to do with that?

PATRICIA (*with a laugh*). Well—you know—open confession is good for the soul—but it's kind of hard on the reputation.

POP (*delighted*). You've got brains, Baby! You take after the Harringtons.

PATRICIA (*with a smile*). Well—I sort of gave in to it—like the man who stole the big safe in a moment of great weakness.

POP. Yes'm—you've got brains, Baby.

PATRICIA. It's lovely of you to say that, Pop.—I hope they never have to open my head to find out. (*Smiles.*)

POP. So Tony's coming here to-night, huh?

PATRICIA. Yes, and I've got to decide something before he gets here, too.

POP. What have you got to decide?

PATRICIA (*rising*). Grace says she's going to marry Tony Anderson. If I marry him and he finds out he could have married Grace—maybe he'd always be miserable. And I'd always be miserable, too—wondering if he was thinking about her. Shall I tell him Grace wants to marry him now or will I marry him myself? (*With a sob.*) Help me, Pop. Help me to decide. What's the sportsmanlike thing to do?

POP. If you love somebody, do your best to get them. All's fair in love and war—don't forget that.

PATRICIA. That's so, isn't it? I forgot that.

POP. You bet your life. Go ahead and marry him, Baby. And when he finds out what a sweet little devil you are he'll forget all about Grace. (*Kisses her head.*)

PATRICIA (*stands a moment in worried thought—looking straight out*). Wasn't Eve a lucky woman ? There was only one man in the world and she had him !

(*Motor is heard in distance.*)

POP (*smiles*). You take Tony and be happy.

PATRICIA (*nods her head*). If he wants me—he can have me !

(*Motor stops.*)

There's Tony's car now. (*Bell.*) Pop ! You go, will you ?

POP (*crossing down and opening door*). Hello, Tony. Come in.

(*Enter* TONY ANDERSON *door* L. *He is in well-cut evening dress and handsomer than ever.*)

TONY (*astonished*). Hello, Mr. Harrington ! Hello, Patricia ! (*Crosses to* C.)

PATRICIA. Hello, Tony ! It was lovely of you to come.

POP. How's Patricia's Park coming along, Tony ?

TONY (*turning to* POP). Great ! Thanks. And I'm glad I happened to see you to-night. Has anybody been around trying to buy your lots ?

POP (*most eagerly*). No. My God, does somebody want to buy them ?

TONY. Yes ; but don't you sell them until I tell you to. You're going to make a lot of money out of those lots.

POP. Yeah ? What's happened ? Who wants them ?

TONY. Keep it a secret if I tell you some good news ?

POP. You bet your life I will—what ?

TONY. I just turned a big deal. I sold part of that tract to some people who are going to put up a $900,000 hotel. Guess where it's going ?

POP (*excitedly*). Anywhere near my lots ?

TONY (*nodding his head—smiling*). Right across the street.

POP (*holding out his hand to* TONY). Gee ! That was darned nice of you to let me in on that, Tony. It'll be the first money I ever made I didn't have to peddle groceries for.

TONY (*happily*). Well, there's no fun making it all yourself—when you have friends who could use a little.

POP. That's right. Well, I've got to leave you youngsters to amuse yourselves. (*Turning up to stairs, winking at* PATRICIA *as he does so.*) I'm working on a very important piece of fiction !

TONY (*very surprised, following him to* R. *of stairs*). You mean you're writing something ?

(POP *looks at* PATRICIA.)

POP. Go on, tell him.

PATRICIA (*laughs*). He's making out his income tax report—getting it ready for next year.

Tony. Well, I hope you'll have a lot more income to report next year.

Pop (*about to go, then turning back*). Thanks.—Oh, say, Tony, it just occurs to me I haven't paid you for them lots yet.

Tony (*laughs*). Oh, that's all right. Wait till you sell them; that's time enough to pay for them.

Pop. You mean pay for them out of the profits?

Tony. Sure——

Pop. That's what I call elegant business——

(*Ad lib. " good nights." Exit up stairs and off* R.)

Tony. What is the trouble you are in?

Patricia (*heaving a sigh*). Tony, something's happened.

Tony (*looking at* Patricia). If there is anything that any man can do—ask me, will you?

Patricia. That's beautiful of you, Tony!

Tony. What is it? Don't be afraid to tell me. Is it something serious?

Patricia. It's something awfully serious to me. It's something I've got to decide—and I want you to help me.

Tony. I'm glad I came—what is it? Something about this fellow you're in love with?

Patricia (*nodding*). Yes—Tony. Tony, I told you he'd been desperately in love with another girl for a long time—— (*Crossing down* R.)

Tony. Yes.

Patricia. And she was engaged to another fellow——

Tony. Yes.

Patricia. Well, she's broken her engagement with this other fellow—and she's telling people that she's changed her mind and is going to marry this one.

Tony (*eagerly*). And this fellow you're in love with has gone back to her, huh? Has he?

Patricia. No. I'd know what to do if that had happened. It's something a lot harder than that to decide.

Tony (*moving to her*). Well, let me help you. I'm disinterested. I'm out of it. I can probably see clearer than you can. What is it?

Patricia. You see—this fellow doesn't know the engagement is broken—and he doesn't know the girl is willing to marry him now.

Tony. And you think when he finds out he'll marry this other girl, eh?

Patricia. Uh-huh. I'm almost sure he will. (*She gives him a wistful, searching look.*) Tony, what would you do—if you were he?

Tony. And he still loves the other girl, eh?

Patricia. Uh-huh. I'm sure he does. Tony, put yourself in his place. What would you do?

TONY (*considers several moments*). Well—I don't know. I'd probably marry this other girl. I hate to be discouraging, Patsy, but I think I would.

PATRICIA (*licked completely. Crossing away*). That's what I think.

TONY (*with new interest*). But what's the problem ?

PATRICIA. Tony, can you imagine a person loving a man so much she'd rather see him happy than to have him herself ?

TONY. Sure I can. That's the way I felt when Grace became engaged to Billy Caldwell. Sure I know.

PATRICIA. Did you, Tony ?

TONY. Sure. I decided if she was happier with him than she'd be with me I wanted to see her marry him.

PATRICIA (*looking at him wistfully*). Yes, you would be like that, Tony ! Tony—the last time I saw this fellow I found out he loves me. He was on the verge of telling me so. In fact, he did tell me. But I'm only second fiddle. He loves me because he thinks he hasn't any chance with this other girl.

TONY (*thoughtfully*). Yeah ?

PATRICIA. Yes. And if I told him I loved him—if I dared to let him find it out—he'd think he wasn't playing fair unless he married me. I know he wouldn't. That's the sort of a fellow he is. That's why I love him.

TONY. You don't want him to find out you love him ?

PATRICIA. No ! Not now ! He'd marry me and then find out he could have married her—and then he'd hate me. Wouldn't he ?

TONY (*considering*). Yes—he probably would ! (*Pause.*)

PATRICIA. Then he'll never find out that I love him. I'd cut my tongue out first.

TONY. I would, too, if I were you, Patsy. I would, too. (*He ponders a moment.*) Still——

PATRICIA. Huh ?

TONY. Good Lord ! This is a problem, isn't it ?

PATRICIA. Tony——   .

TONY. Yes ?

PATRICIA. Do you think if I loved him enough—and was oh, good to him—and tried awfully hard to make him happy—do you think I could make him forget her ?

TONY (*gets up and paces about—his brows knit*). I don't know. It would be terrible to be married to one girl and in love with another.

PATRICIA. Help me to decide, Tony—what's the right thing to do—what's the sportsmanlike thing to do !

TONY. I can't tell you what to do. But I can tell you what I wish you'd do.

PATRICIA. What, Tony ?

TONY. Give this fellow to the other girl. Let her have him.

PATRICIA. Is that what you think I ought to do ?

TONY. Yes, give him to her.

PATRICIA (*with set face, watching his eyes a moment*). All right, Tony, I will. I'll give him to her.

TONY (*impulsively puts his hands on her shoulders and speaks with intense feeling*). Yes, Patricia, let him have her—because I want you! I want you!

PATRICIA (*gasps*). Huh?

TONY (*taking her hands*). I'm in love with you, Patricia. I know it's sudden; but I never realized what sort of a girl you are until lately. I swear I don't believe I even took a good look at you—as long as I've been coming around here. Patricia.

(PATRICIA *turns miserably*.)

I love you, Patricia.

PATRICIA (*miserable—shaking her head—looking away*). No, Tony!

TONY. You mean you can't love me! You can't even try!

PATRICIA (*wretched*). Tony, I'll always remember this as the most beautiful moment—in my whole life—but—I—— (*She shakes her head and her lips compress—unable to trust herself further*.)

TONY (*staring at her for several moments. Slowly picking up his hat, standing holding it a few moments with his back partly toward her*). I don't know what the hell is the matter with me! I don't believe there's a girl in the whole world who gives a damn about me!

PATRICIA (*with her hands clasped at arm's length and straight down and close to her, turns and looks at him with utterly miserable wistfulness*). Oh, Tony!

(*There is the sound of a car outside. The engine stops. Both turn and look toward door. There are heard sounds without. The door opens. Enter* MRS. HARRINGTON *and* GRACE *door* L. *They hold the door open and stop short within, looking at the pair.* MRS. HARRINGTON *farther in,* GRACE *still holding door open*.)

MRS. HARRINGTON. Oh, here you are. (*Sits* L. *of small table*.)
TONY. Hello, Mrs. Harrington!

(*Enter* GRACE.)

GRACE. Huh!
TONY. Hello, Grace.
GRACE. Come on in, Billy.

(*Enter* BILLY. *Crosses to* TONY.)

BILLY. Hello, Tony! Didn't I see you at the dance?
TONY. Yes, but I left.
BILLY. So did we. Grace and I are going out for a little celebration of our own. (*To* MRS. HARRINGTON.) Can I tell them?
MRS. HARRINGTON. I suppose we may.
BILLY. Grace and I have fixed things up. We're going to be married in three weeks, aren't we, darling? (*Trying to kiss her*.)
GRACE. Don't be silly. (*Crossing up to stairs*.) It'll only take me a minute to change my wrap, Billy. I'll be right down.

(*Exit* GRACE *upstairs.*)

BILLY. All right, darling. Isn't she lovely? Sure you won't join us, Mrs. Harrington?

MRS. HARRINGTON. No, thank you, Billy. I must go to bed. I'm ill.

POP (*upstairs—loudly*). Grace—is your mother downstairs?

GRACE (*upstairs*). Yes.

POP (*shouts*). Mrs. Harrington, come upstairs. I want to see you.

MRS. HARRINGTON. If you wish to see me is there any reason why you can't come downstairs to do it?

POP (*firmly*). Did you hear what I told you, May? (*In a commanding voice.*) I says to come upstairs. I want to see you.

MRS. HARRINGTON (*rising, crushed. Bowing as she goes to stairs*). Er—you'll—you'll—— Good night.

POP (*shouts*). May!

MRS. HARRINGTON (*very demurely*). Coming, William! Coming! (*Exit upstairs.*)

(*No one moves till* MRS. HARRINGTON *has gone. All look at each other in astonishment.*)

TONY. Well, Billy——

BILLY. Yes——

TONY. I haven't had a chance to congratulate you, Billy. I wish you both every happiness.

BILLY (*shaking hands*). Thanks, Tony. Thanks.

GRACE (*coming down from stairs*). I'm all ready now, Billy. Come on. (*Starting to door.*)

BILLY. All right, sweetheart. Would you and Pat like to join us, Tony?

TONY. Sorry, but I must be going. Good night, Pat.

(*Exit* GRACE *first—then* TONY, *leaving the door open.*)

BILLY. Good night, Pat.—Don't you think——

GRACE (*off stage*). Billy!

BILLY. Coming, darling.

(*Exit* BILLY.)

(*Motor starts.*)

(TONY *is standing in the doorway, then moves off head down.*)

PATRICIA (*runs to door and calls*). Tony—Tony—Tony. (*Moving up stage.*)

TONY (*enters*). Yes——

PATRICIA (*c. to* L., *her back half turned to him*). Come here, I want to tell you something.

TONY. Yes—— (*Closing the door.*)

PATRICIA (*scared*). Tony! Grace and Billy broke off their engagement—and I didn't know it was fixed up until just now!

TONY. Well?

PATRICIA. Well—(*with a little look at him shyly*)—don't you see?

TONY (*staring at her in astonishment*). Don't I see what?

PATRICIA (*turning and facing him. Very close to him, toying with the lapel of his coat*). Tony,—you know that fellow I'm in love with? The one you said you'd help me to get?

TONY. Good Lord—you don't mean Billy Caldwell?

PATRICIA (*with a gesture of despair*). You said he'd be so dumb he wouldn't know what was going on—but I never would have believed this!

TONY. What are you talking about? Who is it? Who is it?

PATRICIA. I'm going to tell you—but I want to remind you of something first.

TONY. What?

PATRICIA. You said if this didn't turn out all right—if anything happened—you'd remember that you were the one who wanted to try the experiment. You remember that, don't you?

TONY. Yes——

PATRICIA. Tony, the man that I'm in love with is—— (*Heaves a great sigh.—She gives him a quick look and then turns away to await the calamity.*)

TONY (*looks at her amazed a moment*). Who?

PATRICIA (*turning and facing him*). You——

TONY (*stepping back in astonishment*). Huh!

PATRICIA. You're the one you were helping me to win. (*Then turning from him, head down, ashamed.*) Now I suppose you'll hate me.

TONY (*going to her and turning her around*). Listen, Patricia, I've been wanting to ask you a question for the last five days!

PATRICIA. Don't be afraid to ask me, Tony. I've had the answer all ready for the last five years.

TONY (*puts his hands on her shoulders*). Will you——

PATRICIA. Uh-huh! (*She does not answer—just nods her head up and down as she looks straight into his eyes. He pulls her to him and crushing her against him, kisses her. Her arms go impulsively around his neck—clingingly.*)

(POP *comes on to the landing and is about to come downstairs, but on seeing them turns and tiptoes off again.*)

CURTAIN.

Time of representation : 35 minutes.

PROPERTY PLOT

Carpet.
Carpet on stairs and platform.
Long mirror on wall R.—above table.
Curtains over windows.
Pelmets over windows.
Pelmet over clothes cupboard.
Cushion on seats—up C. and windows.
6 shelves of books—prop—library.
In clothes cupboard :
  Row of brass hooks.
  Umbrella-rack.
  Small stand with vase of ferns—on platform.
Large tapestry chair—overstuffed.
Humidor.
Magazine.
Papers.
Large overstuffed tapestry couch.
2 cushions.
4 small books (one with magazine ad.) under cushions
2 small chairs, round backs.
Arm chair L.C., round backed.
Octagon table.
  Ash-tray—magazines.
Large library table (behind couch).
  Telephone on same.
  Magazines—ash-tray—3 empty boxes of candy.
  Book stands—books.
2 console tables.
On same.—2 vases of flowers.
  2 pieces of bric-à-brac.
Baby grand piano.

Stone bench.
Small trellis.
2 hollyhock stands.
Picture on wall—off L.
Door-bell on door—R.

HAND PROPS

Act I

POP.—Travelling-bag.
  Dressing-gown.
  Box of cigars.
  Box of candy.
  Cigars.
  Roll of bills.

BILLY.—Small flower-box.
    Corsage of orchids and lily of the valley.
    Small flask.

Act II

TONY.—Deed.
    Newspaper.
GRACE.—Newspaper.

    Two books are put on small table.
    Large loving cup off R.
    Change flowers.

Act III

MRS. HARRINGTON.—Curling-irons.
POP.—Plate and towel.

ELECTRIC PLOT

X-ray border.—1 circuit of pinks.
  1 circuit of straw.
  1 circuit of white.
Foots.—1 circuit of ambers.
  1 circuit of pinks.
  1 circuit of white.
On stairs off stage.—Small strip.
Off stage—door L.—Small strip.
Off stage—door R.—3 1,000-watts—moonlight blue.
Back of window—up stage.—2 1,000-watts—moonlight blue.
Back of library window.—2 1,000-watts—moonlight blue.
  Can use third border—blues.
Off stage.—Telephone bell.
  Dimmer for auto effect.
  Vacuum cleaner

  1 standard lamp lighted.
  1 table lamp lighted.
  2 wall brackets lighted.
  Remain lit throughout, small lantern in porch.

COCKEYED
William Missouri Downs

Comedy / 3m, 1f / Unit Set

Phil, an average nice guy, is madly in love with the beautiful Sophia. The only problem is that she's unaware of his existence. He tries to introduce himself but she looks right through him. When Phil discovers Sophia has a glass eye, he thinks that might be the problem, but soon realizes that she really can't see him. Perhaps he is caught in a philosophical hyperspace or dualistic reality or perhaps beautiful women are just unaware of nice guys. Armed only with a B.A. in philosophy, Phil sets out to prove his existence and win Sophia's heart. This fast moving farce is the winner of the HotCity Theatre's GreenHouse New Play Festival. The St. Louis Post-Dispatch called Cockeyed a clever romantic comedy, Talkin' Broadway called it "hilarious," while Playback Magazine said that it was "fresh and invigorating."

Winner!
of the HotCity Theatre GreenHouse New Play Festival

"Rocking with laughter...hilarious...polished and engaging work draws heavily on the age-old conventions of farce: improbable situations, exaggerated characters, amazing coincidences, absurd misunderstandings, people hiding in closets and barely missing each other as they run in and out of doors...full of comic momentum as Cockeyed hurtles toward its conclusion."
—Talkin' Broadway

THE OFFICE PLAYS
Two full length plays by Adam Bock

THE RECEPTIONIST
Comedy / 2m, 2f / Interior

At the start of a typical day in the Northeast Office, Beverly deals effortlessly with ringing phones and her colleague's romantic troubles. But the appearance of a charming rep from the Central Office disrupts the friendly routine. And as the true nature of the company's business becomes apparent, The Receptionist raises disquieting, provocative questions about the consequences of complicity with evil.

"...Mr. Bock's poisoned Post-it note of a play."
– *New York Times*

"Bock's intense initial focus on the routine goes to the heart of *The Receptionist's* pointed, painfully timely allegory... elliptical, provocative play..."
– *Time Out New York*

THE THUGS
Comedy / 2m, 6f / Interior

The Obie Award winning dark comedy about work, thunder and the mysterious things that are happening on the 9th floor of a big law firm. When a group of temps try to discover the secrets that lurk in the hidden crevices of their workplace, they realize they would rather believe in gossip and rumors than face dangerous realities.

"Bock starts you off giggling, but leaves you with a chill."
– *Time Out New York*

"... a delightfully paranoid little nightmare that is both more chillingly realistic and pointedly absurd than anything John Grisham ever dreamed up."
– *New York Times*

ANON
Kate Robin

Drama / 2m, 12f / Area

Anon. follows two couples as they cope with sexual addiction. Trip and Allison are young and healthy, but he's more interested in his abnormally large porn collection than in her. While they begin to work through both of their own sexual and relationship hang-ups, Trip's parents are stuck in the roles they've been carving out for years in their dysfunctional marriage. In between scenes with these four characters, 10 different women, members of a support group for those involved with individuals with sex addiction issues, tell their stories in monologues that are alternately funny and harrowing..

In addition to Anon., Robin's play What They Have was also commissioned by South Coast Repertory. Her plays have also been developed at Manhattan Theater Club, Playwrights Horizons, New York Theatre Workshop, The Eugene O'Neill Theater Center's National Playwrights Conference, JAW/West at Portland Center Stage and Ensemble Studio Theatre. Television and film credits include "Six Feet Under" (writer/supervising producer) and "Coming Soon." Robin received the 2003 Princess Grace Statuette for playwriting and is an alumna of New Dramatists.

BLUE YONDER
Kate Aspengren

Dramatic Comedy / Monolgues and scenes
12f (can be performed with as few as 4 with doubling) / Unit Set

A familiar adage states, "Men may work from sun to sun, but women's work is never done." In Blue Yonder, the audience meets twelve mesmerizing and eccentric women including a flight instructor, a firefighter, a stuntwoman, a woman who donates body parts, an employment counselor, a professional softball player, a surgical nurse professional baseball player, and a daredevil who plays with dynamite among others. Through the monologues, each woman examines her life's work and explores the career that she has found. Or that has found her.